Charlotte Carter

DRUMSTICKS

Charlotte Carter is the author of an acclaimed mystery series featuring Nanette Hayes, a young black American jazz musician with a lust for life and a talent for crime solving. Her short fiction has appeared in a number of American and British anthologies. Carter has lived in the American Midwest, North Africa, and France. She currently resides in New York City.

DRUMSTICKS

DRUMSTICKS

A NANETTE HAYES MYSTERY

Charlotte Carter

VINTAGE CRIME/BLACK LIZARD
Vintage Books
A Division of Penguin Random House LLC
New York

FIRST VINTAGE CRIME/BLACK LIZARD EDITION, SEPTEMBER 2021

Copyright © 2000, 2021 by Charlotte Carter
The Library of Congress has cataloged the Mysterious Press edition as follows:
Name: Carter, Charlotte (Charlotte C.).
Title: Drumsticks / Charlotte Carter.
Description: New York : Mysterious Press, c2000.
Identifiers: LCCN 99047073
Subjects: LCSH: African Americans—Fiction. | New York (N.Y.)—Fiction.
Classification: LCC PS3553.A7736 D78 2000 | DDC 813/.54—dc21
LC record available at https://lccn.loc.gov/99047073

Vintage Crime/Black Lizard Trade Paperback ISBN: 978-0-593-31414-2
eBook ISBN: 978-0-593-31415-9

Book design by Christopher M. Zucker

www.blacklizardcrime.com

Printed in the United States of America
10 9 8 7 6 5 4 3 2 1

To the Bennys: Carter, Golson, and Green,
whose songs I love but sometimes mislabel

And in memory of Robert Holkeboer

DRUMSTICKS

CHAPTER 1

'TIS AUTUMN

"UH   NAN? I think we need to go home now."

I stood with my hand on my hip, knocking over several drinks. I looked at him—my little date—with supreme scorn. "Your hands off me, yutz. You go home if you want. Ima have another drink." I know I must've looked ferocious, because a couple of women on the sectional sofa started clawing at the coat sleeves of their men.

"You've had enough, Nan. Let's get your coat." He sounded like Richard Pryor doing his uptight-white-guy accent.

I won't recount what I said to him then. It would make me too ashamed. Just know it was filthy and cruel and utterly uncalled-for. I didn't know I had that kind of poison in me until I heard it rolling off my tongue.

That guy shrank away from me, gasping like a Sunday school teacher in a Storyville whorehouse. I had humiliated his ass in front of his friends—well, I'm guessing they were his friends. Maybe, even worse, they were his colleagues from work, whatever work he did. The truth is, I don't remember what he did for a living; I don't remember what he looked like, except that he was a tall black man who wore nice shirts; and I don't remember whose apartment we were in, because, see, I was drinking pretty heavily then, and had been for months.

And hey, as long as I'm being honest here? To say I was drinking "heavily" is kind of a laughable understatement. The fact is, I was drinking suicidally.

To his credit, my date, whoever he was, turned out not to be such a wimp after all. When my vile, party-killing monologue was over, I began to wend my way back to the table where a gorgeous young sister in dreadlocks and a white apron was serving the drinks. I never made it back there. Before I knew what was happening, my man had a hold of the neck of my shirt. I was thrown out of the front door so hard that I bounced off the back wall of the waiting elevator, landing on my butt. A split second later, my brown suede jacket came sailing in after me, looking for all the world like Rocky the Flying Squirrel.

I cussed all the way down to the lobby, where I stumbled past the tight-lipped doorman, who had undoubtedly watched the whole episode on his security monitor.

It was a Saturday night. I remember that because of all the strolling couples. The ones I looked at with such hatred. The ones whose heads I wanted to saw off because they looked so fucking happy together.

How dare they be happy! How dare they! I wished I had my gun.

And a drink. I wished I had a drink, too.

I'M NOT TRYING to paint myself as a badass or anything—this stuff was nothing to brag about. I was out of control and I knew it.

It had started as a severe post-affair depression last spring, when I returned from Paris. It simmered and deepened over the ugly New York summer, during which I scratched out a living by day—playing my sax long hours on the street and picking up tutoring or translation jobs here and there—and kept to myself at night. I sought the company of no one except for my best friends, Mr. Gin and Ms. Tonic. I kept the answering machine on all the time but rarely returned any calls. Too scattered to read, too listless to write, no hanging with friends, only obligatory contact with my mom and my oldest friend, Aubrey, to let them know I was still alive.

The cooler weather meant a switch to bourbon. In the month of September I drank, if not a river of whiskey, then certainly a major tributary. I also acquired a weapon.

A neighbor of mine had been raped over the Labor Day weekend. The cops thought the guy was responsible for a string of attacks farther uptown as well. In the grip of spiraling nihilism, I purchased an illegal piece, figuring that if he came after me, I'd be the last episode of his series, because I was going to cancel his ass. I fully realized the bastard just might take me with him. But if it came to that—so be it.

I knew a conga player, Patrice, from Haiti, who had kind of a thing for me. Lovely man, but we never quite got our riddims together, to use his words. He had a cousin who specialized in putting people together with the right weapon. Patrice and I made a night of it. He took me first to a Filipino meal on First Avenue; next, to a new club on Avenue A, where a group with a sensational tenor opened for a rising male singer; and last, working our way steadily east, into the bowels of a red brick building on Avenue D.

The cousin, whose name was never mentioned, was one scary fella. But when I emerged onto the street again, I was the proud owner of an only slightly used little Beretta, which, I was told, a former policewoman had traded for heroin. It fit neatly into my hand but was guaranteed to have the punch of a much meaner piece. And, as a bonus, seeing as how I was Patrice's bitch, I was fixed up with regular as well as hollow-point ammo.

Luckily for the both of us, they caught the rapist.

I was walking around in perpetual gloom or hostility or sourness, no gratitude for life and no taste for living. Nothing moved me. And I mean nothing—not the most beautiful tenor solo I heard on the radio, not the heavenly gold and flame that anointed the parks and gardens, not even a good hamburger. My impersonation of Lady Hardass went on. Tough Nan and her beat-up saxophone. She didn't like the way things were, but she bit down on the loneliness and took it like a man.

My friend Aubrey had not given up on me completely; of course not. But she was damned tired of my self-destructive nonsense. We spoke on the phone but seldom got together for dinner or going out to visit my mother—or anything. On the rare occasions when we did meet, we just seemed to get on each other's nerves.

And so November rolled around. I was still depressed, and more evil than ever. I knew it was sheer self-indulgence. But what could I do? And then, one night, I met this guy at a club—I think that's where I met him—and tried to take some solace in a fling with him.

Cut to: that jive party in that deluxe high-rise building, that Saturday night when I went *way* over the top.

Understand, Mr. and Mrs. Hayes did not raise any heathen daughters, and as a person of some refinement, I was unaccustomed to being asked to leave people's homes, let alone being hauled out by the scruff of my neck and tossed into an elevator like I was a crate of lettuce that had gone bad.

Yet I knew I deserved what that guy did to me—and worse. I had behaved abominably.

I got out into the brisk November air, a hint of winter in the wind, and I saw those couples in their big sweaters strolling with their arms around each other. And laughing—that's what really got to me—their sweet, exclusionary laughter. They were done with their little dinners in their little trattorias. They were coming home from the movies. Stopping off for fucking decaf espresso. Going to hear music somewhere where the lights were low. I wanted to kill somebody.

But of course that isn't what I wanted at all. Just the opposite. To be precise, I wanted Andre, the man I had found and then parted from in Paris.

I zipped up my jacket and crossed the street, hurrying up the block and out of the sight of the doorman, now regarding me as if I belonged in a zoo. I barely made it into the doorway of the shuttered cigar store before the dam burst. I broke down and began to sob helplessly. I cried in the way I'd been trying to cry for months, but somehow had not been able to. Mouth wide open, screaming almost, testifying. Snot on my chin. The whole nine yards. I cried so hard and so long that I gave myself a nosebleed.

Scenes like this were regular occurrences in the city: some poor soul, usually a woman, crying her heart out, publicly, past all embarrassment. The pain is almost tangible. You get a sharp, sudden pang of empathy in your throat. You want to cry, too. You start hurting, too. But you don't stop, you don't interfere, you keep walking. And now the poor soul was me; I was the one on display.

Nobody paid me any mind.

At last the storm was over. I was exhausted. I was ravenous. And I was still very sad. But, oddly, I felt a whole lot better. I walked a couple of blocks north and found a no-name diner. While my BLT was being made, I went into the ladies' and cleaned myself up as best I could.

I polished off my sandwich in no time and had a stale cookie with my third cup of coffee. Lord, I thought, I *hope* this is rock bottom—Saturday night, alone in a Greek coffee shop where the most attractive man in sight was gumming a roll that he kept dipping in his watery chicken soup, and me with bloody snot on my good coat and my face looking like a hot air balloon in the Macy's parade. I hope there's nowhere to go but up from here.

It was nearly 2 a.m. when I left the diner. For a brief moment I thought of going back to the party to apologize for my behavior. I quickly scotched that idea. I just knew I didn't want to go home yet. The thought of walking into my empty apartment just then was unbearable. Besides, I owed apologies to somebody else.

I jumped into the first taxi I saw, thanking my stars the cabbie was Indian. They usually pick up black people when nobody else will and it was two in the morning and I looked like I lived under the Brooklyn Bridge.

Under ordinary circumstances the last place on earth I'd want to be at 2 a.m. was Caesar's, the club where Aubrey dances with her tatas hanging out six nights a week. Under ordinary circumstances that loser Greek diner would be preferable to Caesar's Go Go Emporium. But tonight its gaudy neon lights were like a beacon of hope lighting up that bleak patch of Sixth Avenue.

Aubrey was on and it was a full house. Like always, the men were enthralled, loving her moves, eyes riveted on the stage.

I made my way over to the bar, where I saw Justin, the manager, settling in on his reserved barstool. He smiled at me and elbowed a customer off of his stool so that I could sit next to him.

"God amighty!" he said, getting a good look at me. "I hope you caught the license number of that truck."

"I know, I know" was all I said.

"Did you get mugged or something?"

"No, I'm all right."

"Where have you been all this time, Smash-up? Ugly School?"

I laughed in spite of myself, shaking away the runaway tear that was creeping down my nose, and he put a consoling arm around my shoulders. He shook one of his stupid-long cigarettes at me and I took it gratefully.

"Well, even in your bag-lady drag, it's good to see you."

"I've been lying low. Emphasis on 'low.' "

"You got some troubles, right?"

"It's a long story, Justin. And you've heard it a thousand times before. Only the names change."

"Oh, *that*. Say no more, child. Mens! Can't live with 'em, can't chop their pricks off."

He bought me a brandy over my protests that I'd had enough to drink.

We fell silent for a time, until he commented, "Aubrey's still number one," he said, his eyes following her gyrations. "Girl's looking fabulous tonight."

I nodded, and echoed, "Fabulous. And you, Justin. How are you?"

"Little me?" He turned the smile up a notch, then not so much said as sang, "Met somebody noo-hoo."

"No kidding? That's terrific, J." He did look exceptionally happy.

"Still playing your jazz music, Smash-up?"

"Yeah. Still playing. Lot of tourists around this summer. I made out pretty good. I've got to hustle up some kind of steady income soon, though."

"We can always put you in a wig and you can wait tables here. With that shelf of yours, the tips would be awesome. Maybe you could work up some kind of topless routine with your sax. Who knows, darling? Anything goes."

That made me think. Yes, there was a famous lady cellist who played topless. Was the world ready for a topless lady saxophonist? It would sure as hell secure my place in the annals of jazz.

"I'll give it some thought," I said. "How long do you think it'll be before Aubrey's done?"

"A few minutes. Listen, why don't you go backstage to wait for her? I'll be back there in a few minutes."

I grabbed my drink. "Thanks. See you later."

It was nice and warm back in Aubrey's room. I sipped my brandy and picked up her pack of Newports but threw it back down again with a snort of distaste.

I sat at her dressing table and surveyed the damage in the oversized mirror. Yeah. Ugly School. Top of the class. Makeup wasn't going to help much, but I picked up one of Aubrey's lipsticks and began to apply it.

No, I was right; it wasn't helping. Soon I had drawn a pair of terrifying clown lips over my mouth. I popped my eyes wide and sang in falsetto: *"Everybody dance now!"*

I broke into crazy laughter then. It mounted higher and higher, until I became aware that someone else was in the room.

I heard the lifeless greeting: "Hey."

Aubrey was standing behind me, staring at my reflection in the mirror. I whirled around to face her.

"Jesus, Aubrey, I'm sorry. I mean, not just for this. I mean I'm sorry period. About—you know—how I've been."

She stared impassively at me for another few seconds, and then she, too, began to laugh wildly.

I gave her the short version of my earlier humiliation, replete with the frightened women on the sofa and the suede jacket landing on my face. As I should have known, she found that hilarious, too.

Justin found us collapsed in each other's arms.

"What's going on back here, girls? Can I get in on this riot?"

"Yeah, you can," Aubrey said. "You know the party don't start till you come."

He put his crazy cigarette down on the edge of the nearest

surface, and then, with a devilish grin, revealed the object he had been concealing behind his back. "This is for you," he said, looking directly at me. "Happy birthday, Smash-up."

I looked down at it. A twelve-inch-high rag doll with dark brown "skin." And speaking of riots: she was a portly old lady in a wildly colored pinafore and head wrap—jungle reds and yellows and oranges and zebra stripes. On her little face a mysterious expression was sewn in white thread. Her mouth wasn't downturned, exactly, but she certainly wasn't smiling. Her head wrap was color coordinated, to use the term loosely, tightly wound and towering high on her head. There was even a tiny ring in her left ear. And in one hand she held a little pouch with a drawstring.

"That must be where she keeps her voodoo medicine," Aubrey snorted.

"That's right," Justin said, then turned to me to say, "she can put the mojo on that man who jammed you up. You'll get him back in a minute."

"I'm touched, J. But we've got a few months to go before my birthday."

With a toss of his head, he pressed the doll into my hands.

"What the fuck? It's somebody's birthday every day, isn't it? Here, take it. I have it on good authority that this lady will fix up your life, no matter what kind of blues you have. And let's face it, Smash-up, you could use the help."

Like they say, don't look a gift horse in the mouth. Though I never had any idea what that old axiom meant.

"Thanks, J. That's really sweet of you. I think I'll name her Justine, in your honor."

"Uh-uh," he cautioned. "She's already got a name: Mama Lou. You have to call her Mama Lou."

"Okay. But why?"

"*Perry Mason*," he said, as if that answered my question.

"Perry Who?" Aubrey asked.

Myself, I knew who Perry Mason was, but his answer still made no sense.

"You know, that old TV show from the fifties," he began to explain. "He was a lawyer that never lost a case. And my girl Della, his secretary, used to wear these kickass high heels without the backs to them.

"Well, when I first started working at Caesar's, my shift would start about two in the afternoon. So I would get out of bed about eleven or twelve. They used to show *Perry Mason* reruns every day on Channel Five. I would eat my breakfast and get ready for work while I watched it. Got to the point it would ruin my day if I couldn't see it. I saw most of the shows five . . . six . . . a hundred times.

"Anyway, they had this one story about this young white girl who had lost her parents, and so she was raised down in Haiti by this voodoo mammy they called Mama Lou. But somebody killed Big Mama. Man, that was my favorite *Perry*. The thing is, while I was watching it the power went out in my building, and I never found out who the murderer was. They never showed that one again, goddammit. To this day, I don't know who killed Mama Lou.

"So there I am the other day, coming back from Armani on Fifth Avenue, and I cut down Fifteenth Street to come back over east. Right there at Union Square and Fifteenth where all those street vendors hang out—"

"*Armani?*" That was Aubrey's incredulous hoot, interrupting Justin's narrative. "Motherfucker, you don't shop at no Armani and you know it."

He bristled and snapped at the air. "I buy my soap there, bitch. Everybody knows Italian soaps are the best. Anyway, as I was saying, there I am at that corner of Fifteenth and the park. And I look up and there's Mama Lou staring me right in the face.

"There's this woman who looks like she could be a voodoo lady herself. She sews these dolls and sells them on the street there. Got a whole table full of different kinds of dolls. She said all her dolls got magic powers. Hell, I can always use a little magic. So now you come in here looking like . . . well, like you're looking," he said. "I figure you'll be a real good test of Mama Lou's magic. If she can help you, she can help anybody."

I took the doll and held her close, swallowing hard. "From your lips, Justin."

I looked over at Aubrey. "Are you still pissed at me, Aub?"

She didn't say anything, just plucked a few tissues from her table and began to wipe my mouth.

I smiled at the two of them. "Thanks, Mom and Dad," I said.

CHAPTER 2

IT'S MAGIC

THIS FUCKING THING does *not* work!

Two days since Justin had given me the Mama Lou doll and I was damned if I could see any magic changes taking place in my life.

So much for voodoo. So much for Perry Mason.

I had the doll propped up in my saxophone case, so that she could oversee and bless those bills raining into the case as the public showed its grateful appreciation for my playing. Ha. The previous day's take had been mediocre. Today's was downright lousy.

I was blowing in the Times Square station, where any number of musicians I knew from the scene told me they'd been cleaning up as of late. The pickings were supposed to be ripe in Times Square now, owing in great part to the Disneyfication of the area. Hordes of out-of-towners roamed there freely, taking the subways by day and night, no longer afraid of being held up, raped, carjacked, and so on. Little by little, New York is getting rehabilitated as a tourist mecca—that is, becoming a shopping mall, where the real Americans can feel at home.

Like all dyed-in-the-wool Manhattanites, I found the so-called cleanup of Forty-second Street distasteful. What with the pimps, the porn movie houses, the touts for the live sex shows, the drugs, the parasites that hung around the Port Authority terminal, and all the rest of that scuzz, the old Forty-second Street had been no picnic. But it was preferable to this version of Wonderland where everybody was buying inflatable Little Mermaids and queuing up for *The Lion King*.

I had had it with the Deuce. I threw in the towel: packed up and rode to street level on the spanking new escalator.

I'd locked Mama Lou inside the case with a cruel little laugh, hoping she'd suffocate in there.

I walked east, stopping at the main library on Fifth Avenue. I slipped into Bryant Park and crunched around on a few dead leaves, sat down on one of the benches for fifteen minutes or so. Then I went back out onto the pavement to try my luck playing again. Once more I propped up old Mama Lou, my supposed lucky charm.

I got a couple of bucks from some student types, a fiver from a European couple, and assorted coins from the sainted New York types who seem to give money automatically to anybody who asks for it.

After a couple of hours I headed downtown on foot, thinking evil thoughts about the corn-fed tourists in their Kmart jeans; the mayor and his gated-community mindset; lite jazz; turn-off notices; autumn in New York; my bloody karma; and, especially, Mama Lou.

I needed to stop off for groceries. Given the current budget, spaghetti sounded delicious. In the supermarket I walked past the lamb chops and straight to the pasta aisle.

At home, I looked at the Jack Daniel's bottle but didn't go

for it. Instead I kicked out of my shoes and opened a beer. While I made supper, I listened to a Lady Day/Lester tape I've always been fond of, going over to the machine a couple of times to replay "This Year's Kisses."

My tough-guy pose had pretty much dissolved, helped along by that titanic crying fit the other day. I was beginning to feel a little more like myself, kind of human. But I was still broke and I was still sad.

No rush to hear my phone messages. What was the point? I had little desire to talk to anyone. Unless it was Aubrey, I did not plan to return the call. But, just before turning in, I did press the message button and listen.

The voice, a woman's, was vaguely familiar. Not until she said something about a $350 check did I recognize the voice to be that of the secretary at the travel magazine where I work periodically, translating articles from French into English. Apparently, through some computer mix-up, they had the wrong address for me. They had been sending me the same check, and getting it back in the mail, for weeks.

Money! At last, a piece of good luck.

I sent up a little prayer of thanks and a silent apology to Justin. If he had such great faith in the silly doll, then I guess I could give her a little credit, too.

Actually, Mama Lou was not the first doll I owned as an adult. I used to keep some West African cuties on a shelf in the kitchen, but I ditched them when I last repainted the apartment—ended up giving them to a neighbor's little girl.

I used to tell all my secrets to my dolly when I was a kid. In fact, if memory serves, my father caught me whispering tearfully to her once. Naturally he insisted on knowing what I was telling her. I'm sure I lied to him. Daddy wasn't big on superstitions or black people who fell under their sway. Lucky charms, Friday the thirteenth, dream books, avoiding ladders and cracks in the sidewalk. All nonsense, he said. Work hard, eat right, do the honorable thing, and you won't need luck.

But I did. I needed a lucky break.

FOUR DAYS A WEEK, the north quadrant of Union Square Park was converted into a farmers market—a heady mix of ravishing wild-flowers, spices, craft works, and seasonal produce. Twenty varieties of apples and squash and arcane hybrids of potatoes; pumpkins as big as a Volkswagen, homemade pies, sheepskin blankets, and brick oven focaccia; hand-churned butter and organic honey—an endless list of goods that city folks craved and were prepared to pay dearly for. By night, the same patch of the park became a gathering place for teenagers polishing their Rollerblading skills.

So, the question was, Did I really need that bunch of gritty broccoli rabe, or was I inventing an errand just so I could get a look at the doll's creator, the real-life Mama Lou?

With the bustling market on my left, I walked and scanned the skinny strip of Broadway—or Union Square West, as the new street sign was calling it—running along the park. There was a vitamin store at the corner of Seventeenth, and next to it, a McDonald's. I'd always liked that.

A few doors down, there was a pissy wine shop, and then the terraced seafood restaurant where middle-aged lovers liked to gather on summer nights.

I continued south. Past the hugely successful all-night coffee shop where the younger crowd flocked, naively hoping to spot a few supermodels out for their midday yogurt and heroin.

Finally, Fifteenth Street. That was where the dolls were sold, Justin had said. I'll be damned, there they were! A bevy of dark dolls dressed in riotous colors. The folding table, set up in front of the office building with a bank on the ground floor, was thick with them. And the real Mama Lou was at her place, on a metal chair. No customers around, she was playing solitaire at one edge of the table.

I didn't go up to her right away. Instead I looked at the goods on the unattended folding table next to hers, which contained a sea of unctuous body musk in dark glass vials. Some people find those scents sexy, I think. I don't get that.

"He'll be back in a minute, honey," the doll lady said, placing a ten of hearts on the jack of spades. "I'm watching his stuff for him."

"Oh, that's okay," I said. "I'm just looking."

A black man with matted hair, who had been dozing near the entrance to the ATM, roused himself and approached me, paper cup extended.

I gave him a buck, but when he wanted to engage me in one of those panhandler flirtations, I shook him off and sauntered over to the doll lady's table.

"What's the matter?" she said with a teasing laugh. "Don't you need a new boyfriend?"

"Funny you should ask," I said. "As a matter of fact, I do. Since I can't get the old one back."

"Oh, you'll get him, honey. Just let me know if his grand-daddy is single."

We had a good laugh together.

"What's your name, baby?" she said.

"Nan."

"I'm Ida Williams."

She swept all the cards together then, ending the game. I looked at her ebony hands, nimble even though they were old, with knuckles like little marbles.

"You've got some worries on your mind, huh?" she said.

I was taken aback. "Does it show?"

She didn't answer.

"I guess I haven't been having the best luck lately with— well, with anything."

"Um-hum. Well, that's going to change."

"You think so?"

"Everything in its time, honey, everything in its time."

Mrs. Williams patted my hand then. I was crying, and I hadn't even known it.

Three young women laden with shopping bags walked up to the table just then. A lucky thing that they did. Because otherwise I might have unloaded my worried mind on Mrs. Williams. Which would have been incredibly dumb. I'd known the woman for all of five minutes. There was just so much empathy in those old eyes of hers. She was friendly and funny and salty. But, oddly enough, there seemed to be sadness in her as well.

The potential customers began examining Ida's wares. She went into her spiel and I stepped aside.

"Nice to meet you," I called to her as I began to walk away.

"All right, you have a beautiful day, honey."

I looked back, more than a little skeptical.

"Just look up," she added. "See? It's already beautiful, isn't it?"

She was right. I removed my scarf and let the strong sun play on the back of my neck. It felt wonderful.

I COULD DO no wrong.

Yesterday was yesterday. Today, I could do no wrong. Or should I say "we" could do no wrong. The Mama Lou doll sat there beaming with pride while I played my ass off.

I had planned to play outside the big soulless café on Fifty-third Street and Seventh Avenue for only an hour or so and then head back downtown. But the crowd wouldn't let me go. The case was fat with dollar bills.

One nattily dressed older man, hammered on martinis by the smell of things, had me play "Save Your Love for Me" three times. With every rendition he would drop another ten-dollar bill. When he was young, he said, he had a terrible crush on Nancy Wilson. He was staying at the Sheraton, which was just across the street, by the way, if I was interested.

Then a lady in a fur asked if I knew Stevie Wonder's "Ribbon in the Sky." Not really. I bumbled my way through it. Ten bucks from her, too.

Your girl was money that day.

I finally did close up shop, put the loot in my wallet, and walked to the nearest station for the downtown Lex.

Maybe I ought to buy Mama Lou a fur, I thought as the train whipped along. Keep her warm all through the winter.

At the Twenty-third Street station I took the stairs two at a time. And practically floated up the stairs to my apartment.

That night's phone message beat the one from the magazine by a mile: my old music coach, Jeff Moses, was phoning to say he had a regular gig for me, if I wanted it. I would be filling in for an ailing saxophonist, part of a trio that played three nights a week at a restaurant uptown.

Damn right I wanted it.

I ran over to my instrument case, tore Mama Lou from her prison, and gave her a big wet kiss.

"GOOD AFTERNOON, Mrs. Williams." I greeted the thin, dark-skinned woman, who today was wearing a red windbreaker over her brightly patterned dress.

"How you today, honey?" she answered with a smile.

"I'm fine. Much better. And I just wanted to thank you."

She furrowed her brow.

"Let me explain," I said. "A friend of mine gave me one of your dolls a few days ago. Like you said, I've had a lot of worries. But my luck has totally changed."

"Well, of course," she said. "These dolls have got some powers, girl. Powers we don't even know about."

"I'm sure you're right, Mrs. Williams. And by the way, do you make all these yourself?"

"Just call me Ida. Yes, I make them. Each one is different, see, just like us. But they all have the power. And I'll tell you something else about 'em, baby. They only work when you ready for them to work. So you musta been ready."

As she talked, she was subtly moving a couple of the dolls forward on the table surface. "Of course, some are a little more special than others. Look at this one here."

"She's beautiful," I said, "and she looks like she means business, too."

"She" was a tall and lanky black one—a kind of mamba priestess in an intense blue sarong and orange headdress. There was a circle of wire at her neck and she wore an ankle bracelet. She, too, carried a little medicine pouch.

Ida picked up the doll and pressed her into my hands. "Now I'm not saying the one you have can't bring you what you need to be happy. But with this one, honey, you could rule the world."

Quite a claim.

I had been playing my belief in Mama Lou for laughs, more or less. Even Justin's credence seemed a bit tongue-in-cheek.

Was it possible that Ida's faith in her creations was the real thing—that she actually believed what she was saying?

"How much?" I asked.

"She's a really special one, remember. But for you . . . eighteen-fifty."

Ida couldn't possibly support herself by selling these, I was thinking; I mean, realistically, even on the best day, how big is the demand for voodoo picaninnies? But on the other hand, she was a very smooth saleswoman. If she was able to play everybody else as deftly as she was handling me—well, maybe there was enough in it to cover the rent.

I pulled a twenty from my money belt and told her to keep the change.

"You are a sweet thing," she crooned. "Just you wait and see what kinds of good things are gon' come to you."

I was halfway across the park. But then I turned back and ran over to her table again. "I want to invite you someplace, Ida. I'd like you to come as my guest."

"Me? Where you want to invite me?"

"To hear me play. You like music, don't you?"

"Do I look like I don't? We wouldn't be nothing without music."

I wrote down the address of the restaurant where my three-day-a-week gig was to take place and told Ida I would leave her name with the host up front.

"This sounds like a pretty fancy place."

I shrugged and made a motion with my hand that signified "Don't worry about it."

"That's okay with me, girl. I got a dress that'll knock 'em out."

I laughed. "Cool, Ida. I can't wait to see it."

"What kind of music you play—piano?"

"No. Sax. I'm in this trio."

"Lord, if that don't beat all. I bet your mama and daddy real proud of you. Will they be there?" she asked.

I smiled. "Not this time."

I put the second doll in my case, so that Mama Lou wouldn't be lonely. I just hoped she wouldn't be jealous.

————

I TOOK PAINS, usually, to avoid Soho.

But I did have that $350 windfall, and the restaurant where I was going to be playing was kind of grown-up/dress-up, and there was that one nice shop on Prince Street that sold some of the world's greatest black skirts—black chiffon skirts with lace overlays; black wool skirts slit up to where even your doctor shouldn't be looking; ballgown-length black taffeta skirts; tight ones, long ones, short ones. I like them all. So when I left Ida, I set off straight down Broadway to find something to wear to the gig.

My luck was holding. I even found a quarter on the ground.

I didn't hang on to it for very long, though. Before I reached Eighth Street, an aged, pitiful-looking drag queen with big old feet hit me for money. It didn't even occur to me not to comply. I gave her the quarter and all the rest of the change I had in my pockets.

I was getting arrogant—spreading my good luck around.

CHAPTER 3

REPETITION

THE AUDIENCE AT OMEGA, an upscale eatery way up on First Avenue, came primarily to eat, not to hear the music. Jeff had told me that from the git. But the clientele was too sophisticated to treat us as mere white noise; there would be plenty of diners who knew the difference between elevator jazz and the real deal.

In other words, it was unlikely I was going to be discovered and whisked into the recording studio by the kind of scout who haunts the neighborhood basketball courts or the comedy clubs looking for fresh meat. But I did have to have my stuff together to play with the consummate professionals who were to be my fellow musicians.

Roamer McQueen is the cutest fat guy I ever met. He is a talented bassist and, from what I could gather, the heart and soul of the trio that gigged three days a week at Omega. He was extremely kind to me in those rushed, nerve-racking days when I was rehearsing with him and Hank Thayer, the elegant pianist at the center of the group. In fact, they were both wonderful to me.

For whatever reason, men seem compelled to come up with pet names for me. Roamer had dubbed me Big Legs. Canny showman that he was, he promised me a juicy solo for every low-cut blouse I wore to the gig. He is a riot.

I was subbing for sax player Gene Price, the third Musketeer, whose penchant for cheese grits and filterless cigarettes had him in the hospital for bypass surgery.

If I have to say so myself, I looked incredible in that button-up-the-back number I bought on Prince Street. Before I left the apartment that night, I asked Mama Lou and Dilsey (that is what I named the new doll) to work their special hoodoo to bring me good fortune at the gig. I blew each of them a kiss as I breezed out the door. I hopped right on the First Avenue bus, whistling "Liza" as most of the sentient males checked me out on the long seat at the back. Men. *Meh.* Doing fine without em, I thought. I was riding pretty damn high.

Yeah, real high. Once again I was making the mistake of not paying attention to another old black female figure in my life. Her name is Ernestine and—being my stern if quixotic conscience—she can be a real pain in the butt. Ernestine doesn't seem to like it very much when I'm riding high. I'm sure she was trying to warn me, but that night I just wasn't listening.

They fed us at the restaurant; that was part of the deal. And the food wasn't bad. Certainly it was better than the pay. But in any case I was too keyed up to eat.

Both Aubrey and Justin were working that night and couldn't make the set, but they had promised to come see me later in the week.

I'd miss them, sure, but the one I found myself so looking forward to seeing was Ida Williams, the doll lady. It was almost like having your eccentric grandmother out there cheering for you on opening night.

I had gotten into the habit of dropping off containers of hot tea at her table every time I was in the vicinity of the farmers market. Sometimes Ida looked like the tough old bird and master salesperson I had first encountered, and sometimes she seemed frail as parchment, distracted and rueful. Complicated, in other words. I was hoping that someday soon I could talk my mom into coming into the city so that the three of us could go out to lunch.

I had been told that Omega did well. No lie, apparently: The ordinarily supercool maître d' was overwhelmed. People were pouring in. Drinks flowing. A good buzz in the room. Omega was a far cry from some smoky basement club where Monk and Charlie Rouse or Art Tatum or Max Roach was about to make history and (*your favorite brilliant junkie horn player's name here*) was out back scoring a nickel bag. But what the hell? This was still fun. I was still riding high.

The first set started at nine. Hank had a pretty arrangement of "Stella by Starlight" that was to open the set. The three of us stood schmoozing on the slightly raised platform near the front window of the restaurant.

In the midst of the throng of customers I spotted Ida talking to the coat check lady, who was helping her with her wrap.

Go on, Ida! Wow, what a dress. Classic chic-lady-out-cabareting threads. I wondered if she had found it in one of the expensive antique clothing stores in town, or if it was a number she'd been keeping in mothballs since the fifties. Understated nubby wool, clinging in all the right places, too. As Justin would say, not a sequin in sight. Plus, she had done her hair up in a fabulous finger wave.

I broke into a grin and waved hello, but she was too far away. She didn't see me. The small table near the bandstand was all arranged for her, and I was just about to step down to thank her for coming and find out what she wanted to drink. But that never happened.

The room suddenly exploded.

Gunfire and shrieks of terror.

Customers and staff alike went diving for the floor. I felt Hank's fingers around my wrist. He snatched me under the piano seat and my saxophone went bumping off the bandstand.

It was all over in a few seconds. There was confused disbelief on every face in the room: no, the sky wasn't falling; no, we weren't being robbed of our jewels by a band of masked brigands; no, the lunatic terrorists were not herding us into the back room. None of that.

Then what the fuck had just happened?

Roamer and Hank were on their feet again, brushing off their suits and exchanging confounded looks.

I remembered then. Ida!

I hoped she hadn't been trampled in all the confusion.

I ran to the maître d's station, where a knot of people were staring down at the floor in horror, all the women in the group with their hands at their mouths.

Ida.

One perfect hole in the middle of her face. A pool of bloody goo under her head.

I dropped to the floor and began a frantic check for any signs of life. Useless. I let out a dreadful deep moan that soon shot up into the high register. After that, I must've spaced out completely—gone somewhere deep in my own head. I went into some sort of trance and I didn't come out of it until I felt Roamer and Hank leading me to a chair.

"Oh no," I wailed, over and over. "Not again."

CHAPTER 4

BLACK COFFEE

THE COPS DETAINED US for an eternity at Omega while they dusted and photographed, yammered on their walkie-talkies, conducted their interviews, took witness statements, such as they were, and oversaw the removal of Ida's body.

Of course I came in for a particular grilling, because I was the only one on the premises who knew the murder victim—however vaguely. A uniformed officer plopped me down at a table for four near the kitchen, separating me from Roamer and Hank.

Ida had thirty bucks or so in her small handbag, a lipstick, mirror, comb, cigarettes, coin purse. But no wallet—no identification. The detective in charge, Loveless, for some reason found it difficult to believe I had no idea what Ida's address was, whether she had family in the area, children, how old she was, and so on. After all, he pointed out, Ida was there at my invitation.

I told him I knew her only as a neighborhood street vendor who had been nice to me and from whom I'd purchased a "rag doll." Because she had been so pleasant, I explained, I had on the spur of the moment invited her to hear me play. I was damned if I'd tell that overweight, phony macho *NYPD Blue* wannabe about Ida's dizzy superstitions, not to mention my own.

The futile questions went on and on, as did the promises that it would only be another few minutes. And the minutes ticked by and turned into hours. For a while there, I really thought I was going to lose it. Even the gruff Lieutenant Loveless could see that I was ready to pull my hair out by the roots.

I'm sure he thought I was just another in the long line of women with the vapors, freaking out about what had happened. He was wrong.

True, poor Ida lying in that bloody mess was a horror. The thing was, it wasn't the first time I'd seen something like that. Before I left Paris the previous spring, I'd seen my aunt Vivian—my own flesh and blood—in spookily similar condition, lying dead through the worst kind of violence.

To see the same thing played out all over again was just too much. It was almost unbelievable. And maybe that's why I had no tears left for sweet Ida Williams.

The Bad Lieutenant as much as told me he figured Ida just "caught a tough break"—that some idiot had stormed into the restaurant not intending to kill anybody but only to scare the hell out of this roomful of fat cats, but unluckily for Ida, his aim wasn't so good.

"You should know," he said. "You were standing up there. You saw what happened."

"I certainly did not," I informed him, for the hundredth time. "Maybe some of the witnesses say they *think* they saw the policeman's favorite citizen. But I never did."

"What does that mean—the policeman's favorite citizen— what is that supposed to mean?"

"That ubiquitous black man who does everything when nobody's looking. He kidnaps little children, he hijacks vegetable trucks, he fucks up the Internet—just causes no end of trouble for law-abiding people."

His face was a mask. Not a jot of appreciation for my wit. "Okay. So you didn't see anything. As soon as you took the first step down from the bandstand, all hell broke loose. But you did hear the shots. Three of them. Two went wild and the other one killed the victim."

The victim. The victim. God, I wished he'd stopped using that cold, anonymous phrase. Her name was Ida Williams. But then, whenever I looked over at the figure in the black plastic bag, *victim* seemed an all too apt description.

"Sure, it's possible," Loveless admitted a few minutes later. "Could be the shooter did come in with murder on his mind."

But if so, he pointed out impatiently, "it wasn't that woman he meant to take out. Maybe he didn't expect to find such a huge crowd and he got spooked or something. Maybe somebody jostled him and made his shots go wild. Maybe he didn't realize how dark it would be in here. He just missed his man, or woman, as the case may be. If somebody did this on purpose, it wasn't that old lady who was supposed to get it. It was a mistake."

Why? I wanted to ask. Wasn't Ida Williams important enough to be killed for herself?

Loveless must have been reading my mind, or at least reading my sour expression. He asked me dutifully, "*Did* she have any enemies?"

Of course I had no answer for him. But that didn't stop me. No, Motormouth Nan couldn't let it go. "We've all got enemies," I said tartly. "What about you, Lieutenant? Does the whole world love you?"

His incinerating look shut me up momentarily. I knew I was mouthing off when I should've been playing it cool—just taking things in, observing. Besides, common sense made me concede that Loveless was probably right. Ida was just in the wrong place at the wrong time.

"Look, missy," he finally said with a sigh. "You seem to be telling me two opposite things here. One, you're telling me the vic was a nice old lady who sold toys on the street, like something out of a fairy tale. You can't imagine she would hurt a fly. But then you turn around and insinuate that I'm not taking her seriously as a candidate for a paid hit. You can see my problem with your attitude here, right?"

I didn't say anything. He had me there.

That didn't mean his view of Ida's death as a kind of freak occurrence was not full of maddening condescension.

But he did have me.

"You been working here long?" Loveless asked then, softening a bit.

I shook my head. "No. This was my first and maybe last night. I was filling in for a musician who's sick."

"Guess you caught a nasty break, too," he said. I waited while he tapped a ballpoint on his notepad. "You know the owner of this place?" he asked mildly.

"Not really. I've seen him a few times."

"Nice guy?"

"I guess. Nice enough to me. He likes music."

"Well, that's just peachy," Loveless said. "Listen, Miss Hayes, if anybody was going to get whacked here tonight, the manager's a much likelier target than your friend."

That's when I turned off the motormouth.

"Yeah, Mister Nice Guy has got a history of borrowing money for his business ventures. Some people, you borrow money from them and don't pay it back on time, it makes them kinda upset. You get what I mean?"

I nodded my complete understanding.

"And some of the other employees around here, Miss Hayes," he continued, "the bouncer, for example. You think a big ugly guy like that is a stranger to the department? Why don't you ask him sometime about the accommodations at some of our finer state institutions?"

I cast a surreptitious look over at the bulk of Nate, to whom I had never paid a minute's notice before. "Gotcha," I said.

"So understand, Miss Hayes. We're not making any accusations here. I still think the person who shot up this place was some kind of a nut. But what I *don't* think is that an old lady who sells dolls in Union Square Park is at the top of anybody's hit list."

He paused there, and when he spoke again, he said, "You know, I think I could see somebody wanting to whack you. We could start looking into your life. How'd you like that?"

That tore it.

"Thanks very much," I said. "I think I'll pass on that."

The Bad Lieutenant lit a cigarette then. "We'll be in touch."

IT WAS MUDDY DAWN before I got home. I had not slept at all. Now, in the morning light, I looked down into the heavily weeded courtyard and saw the super's scruffy old dog nosing into a Kentucky Fried Chicken bag.

My coffee was ready—the second pot. I poured myself some, spiking it liberally with bourbon. I wrapped up in a blanket, then took to the couch. Grim and alone. Again.

Ida Williams had been so busy pushing those goddamn dolls to everybody else that she forgot to keep one for herself.

And as for my luck—well, that didn't last long, did it? After being all messed up behind everything that had happened in Paris, after being miserable and drunk for months, it looked like my luck had finally turned. I'd stopped boozing. Rejoined the human race. I'd got back on track with Aubrey. I'd got into a nice groove on the street, making nice money. I'd even got a job I could stand. Yet, here I was again.

Sure enough, the old karma was still working, still kicking my butt.

I groaned. The newspapers would be out now. Some of the late editions might very well carry the story of what had happened at Omega last night. It was quite possible that Jeff, who had gotten the gig for me, might be reading about it in a couple of hours' time—or Justin might see the story, or, God help me, my mother. What if the papers mentioned my name, listing me as a friend of the victim? I groaned a second time.

As I had given the police what scant information they had on Ida, there was a very good chance I'd be mentioned. I could just imagine Mom browsing through the *Daily News* over her morning Taster's Choice and spotting my name.

About thirty minutes later, the phone rang. Once *maman* calmed down sufficiently to hear me out, I confessed.

So now she knows how I spend my nights. Actually it was a relief—I was happy not to be deceiving her about it anymore.

But as for the other huge lie I was living with, namely that I taught French part-time at NYU, I think if that venerable institution ever burned down, I'd rather assume a new identity—let her think my charred remains were buried in the rubble—than cop to the truth.

I pulled out the telephone cord after Mom's call. I'd leave messages for Jeff and Aubrey later in the day. Right then, all I wanted to do was sleep.

Easier said than done. I gave up after an hour and pulled myself out of bed. I bathed and dressed and then went out in search of breakfast.

It took a long, long time for the coffeehouse explosion to hit my nabe. But once it did, it hit with a vengeance. A couple of years ago we had only the old-fashioned Greek diners or the pricey full-service restaurants. Low end, high end. Almost nothing in the middle. I guess the Starbucks craze kicked the new trend into gear. Thank you, Seattle. There are now half a dozen civilized cafés, each with its own personality, where you can get a real espresso or latte. In a couple of them, they even let you have a cigarette.

I grabbed both *Newsday* and the *Daily News* from the outdoor rack at the magazine store on Third Avenue and turned into the first café I came to.

My name wasn't exactly in twenty-point type. I saw "Nanette Hayes of Manhattan" buried somewhere in paragraph three of the *News* reportage, and no mention at all of me in the other paper. I pushed my cinnamon roll aside and went back to the beginning of the story.

True, as reported, an unknown assailant at a crowded, fashionable Upper East Side restaurant had murdered a sixty-ish black woman who made a living as a craftsperson/street vendor . . . "selling hand puppets." Well, they were slightly off on that part.

"Restaurant patrons interrogated at the scene were unable to give investigators a description of the gunman. Differing accounts of the incident have left police with no clear picture of who might have been responsible for the shooting.

"Lieutenant Frank Loveless said that no motive for the killing had surfaced. For the moment police are working under the assumption that the murder was a tragic accident and that Ida Williams was an innocent bystander," the story concluded.

Right again. Though the lieutenant had not used such delicate language with me. I had no memory of his using the word *tragic*, or *innocent*.

I ordered another coffee. I was giving my poor body all kinds of mixed signals. Tired and wired at the same time. But I no longer wanted to sleep; whenever I closed my eyes now I saw that nasty hole in Ida's forehead.

Two shots went wild, the Bad Lieutenant had said, and the third killed the victim. Talk about rotten luck. Two bullets wind up in the wall—wild, indeed—but the final one hits Ida so squarely in the face it's as if someone decided to see what she'd look like with a third eye.

Well, I was making an unwarranted assumption there, wasn't I? Who was to say that it was the third and final shot that killed Ida? Maybe it was the first.

Maybe that wily bastard Loveless was correct. Maybe Ed Brubeck, who owned Omega, was in with some dangerous people and they decided to get even with him for welching on a debt. But those people don't send out guys who can't shoot straight. If Ed was the target, why didn't the killer walk into his office and waste him? Or get him as he stepped out of his car?

Brubeck was nowhere in sight when the mayhem began.

Nowhere in sight. How did I know that?

Because when I waved to Ida, I did have a couple of seconds to see who was standing nearby. Several customers. The coat check lady. Ida herself. But not Ed Brubeck. He was in his office, at the back of the restaurant and down a flight of stairs. Nate the bouncer was nowhere near either.

And yet— Oh shit, I thought, I don't know. Lieutenant Loveless had all the reason on his side. His wrong place, wrong time theory was supremely rational.

So why couldn't I accept it?

I had the unhappy answer to that one—rather, Ernestine did: I couldn't accept it because if it had not been for me, Ida would never have been in that place at that time.

It wasn't my fault she was dead. Yeah. I know. I had nothing to do with the murder. But I felt partly responsible. Why?

Because I couldn't just leave well enough—or bad enough—alone. I couldn't keep my nose out of Aunt Vivian's business and I couldn't just buy the stupid doll from Ida and walk away. I had to befriend her, impress her. I was riding too goddamn high. And now she was dead. Just like Vivian.

I arrived back home feeling as low as ever, notwithstanding the buzz I had from all that coffee. My eye fell immediately on the two dolls, my new friends. My luck. They were going to turn my life around, remember? They seemed to be laughing at me now. Well, it served me right for buying into that superstitious bull.

I pulled out my sax and farted around with a couple of the numbers I had rehearsed with Hank and Roamer.

But what was the good of that? We would not be playing tonight. And not for some nights to come, if I was guessing right. The cops had sealed Omega as a crime scene.

At least I did one good deed—only one. I avoided the thing that would probably have finished me off. I did not start drinking.

What I did do, I grabbed Mama Lou and Dilsey by their necks and threw them into the trash basket beneath the desk.

Something was wrong. Something was just so wrong. And voodoo had nothing to do with it.

CHAPTER 5

FILTHY MCNASTY

"AW . . . AW NAW! What the fuck do *you* want?"

The expression on his face—terror meets contempt—was priceless. And the white paper napkin tucked into his shirt collar didn't hurt the picture.

I gave him a thousand-watt smile. "I just called to say I love you, Leman."

He did not laugh.

But then, as I remembered all too well, Leman Sweet was a man with very little laughter in him. He was a massive presence with close-shorn hair. In the time since we'd last met he had eighty-sixed the dumb Fu Manchu mustache he wore then and traded it for a bristle-brush one too diminutive for his thick lips and massive jaw.

"Don't be calling me Leman, Cueball."

He wagged a finger at me. His hand was the size of an Easter ham.

I winced at hearing his favorite name for me, a reference to the days when I wore a shaved head.

"As far as you're concerned, Cueball," he said, "Sergeant is my first name and Sweet is my last name."

"Whatever," I said mildly. "May I join you?"

"Can I stop you?"

Tough call. I didn't know the law. Was it a crime to pull up a chair at a person's table in a family-style barbecue joint?

"I guess you expect me to ask you to lunch, too," he grumbled, wiping at the sauce on his chin. "You got more nerve than a little, if I remember right."

Leman Sweet, not the most gracious black man I knew, was running true to form. He was busting my chops thoroughly.

And in fact that is how our strange relationship, shall I call it, began. Detective Sweet of the NYPD had been one of the first officers to arrive on the scene very late one night when a singularly unpleasant thing occurred in my apartment: another cop—undercover, posing as a down-and-out musician—was murdered on my kitchen floor.

What's more, the dead cop had been Sweet's partner. *I* didn't kill him, needless to say. I had been used in a brutal way by some pretty brutal people, and nearly wound up dead myself. But Sweet, who had taken an instant dislike to me, needed to blame somebody for his partner's death, and he had elected me.

That had happened long ago. At least it seemed like ancient history to me. I never expected to see Detective Sweet again as long as I lived—let alone that I'd be tracking him down, interrupting his mega-calorie lunch, and about to ask him for advice *and* a favor.

"I'm not hungry, thanks," I told him. "I was just wondering if you could spare a few minutes."

He grunted. "How did you know I was here, anyway?" he asked.

"I called your old precinct. They told me you had been transferred to a special unit on Twelfth Street. When I went up there, the desk sergeant said you were at lunch and he thought you usually ate someplace on Eighth Street. The smell of pork eliminated most of the other prospects around here. That, and the number of black folks I could see chowing down when I looked in through the window."

He gnawed greedily at a blackened bone. "Well, ain't you the slick detective?"

"I can also deduce by the pile on your plate that you must've ordered the $8.95 combination platter."

He pushed his plate away then and fixed me with a direct look. "Okay, Cueball. You showed off your smarts. Now, like I said before, what do you want with me?"

"First of all, I need you to listen to something. Just listen. And then tell me what you think. Here, let me get you another Coke."

I began with the gift of the Mama Lou doll and took the narrative all the way through my interrogation at Omega—even admitting in the process that I had fallen for Ida's promises of good luck and riches if I believed in Mama Lou's and Dilsey's powers. It took some effort to spill that last part; I was pretty embarrassed by my foolishness.

When I looked up, Sweet was regarding me not so much with hostility as with scornful pity.

"So?" I said humbly.

"So?"

"So can you help me out? Help me find out if somebody murdered Ida. And even if they didn't, even if it was an accident, help me find out who she was and if she had any family. They ought to be notified. I don't want her to end up in Potter's Field like some kind of tramp."

"What the hell do you think the police are for, girl? They're going to find all that out."

"Yes, I assume they will. But that cop Loveless has already made up his mind about the case. Loveless is not going to investigate with any—I don't know—enthusiasm. He's too busy trying to look like that TV cop with the mustache and the tight suits. And whatever he finds, he's not hardly going to keep me in the loop. Ida means nothing to him. And neither do I."

"Loveless does his job. Better than most of them. And don't you say nothing about that show or Dennis Franz."

"You mean you know him? I don't mean Dennis Whosis, I mean Loveless."

"I met him. He's a solid cop. And you lucky he didn't pop you upside your head for being such a smartass with him."

"Yes, I can see now how lucky I was," I said, unable to push my irritation down any longer. "I'm familiar with your charming investigative techniques, Sergeant. I remember how you extract confessions from your suspects. How you banged me around when we first met."

"Don't press it, Cueball."

I took a deep breath and backed down, shaking off the powerful sense memory of his sweat as he shoved me down onto my sofa and loomed over me like the dark alter ego of Barney, that fuzzy purple icon of the preschool set.

Better listen to him, I told myself, don't press it. You need his cooperation, bad.

"Okay, so you kind of know Loveless, right? That's a good thing, right? He might tell you what they've found out. Will you call him? Tell him there's something fishy about the way Ida was shot?"

"But he told you, there *ain't* nothing fishy about it. Who says there is—Mama Lou?"

"Ha fuckin' ha. Maybe she did, Leman—I mean, Sergeant. But even if I'm crazy to take the doll stuff seriously, that doesn't mean the story doesn't smell. It was just too convenient, the way she was shot. I can feel it. Will you call Loveless—please?"

He didn't answer right away. In fact, he didn't answer at all. "Why you always gotta think you know better than the pros?" is what he said.

"I don't. Believe me, I don't. I'm just trying to do what's right. Suppose—just suppose someone did kill that old woman. Do you want them to get away with it? You think it's right to just sweep another black body under the carpet?"

"Don't talk that shit to me, girl. I know more about black people dying in this town than you ever dreamed of. You don't know shit."

"All right," I said, calm again. "All right, I know you do. But I have to find some way to put this to rest, man. I'm just feeling so guilty."

"About that woman? Don't be stupid. It wasn't your fault."

My God, what was this? Compassion from Leman Sweet? A tiny ray of ordinary human kindness—for me? It left me speechless.

"Look," Sweet said, cleaning his fingers with the Wash'n Dri he took out of its foil wrapper, "maybe something smells, and maybe it doesn't. But either way, I don't have no business sticking my nose in Loveless's case—and more to the point, no time. Right now I'm swamped with another case where the powers that be are sweeping a black carcass under the rug. A lot more than one carcass, matter of fact."

"What are you talking about? Serial killings?"

"You could put it that way. I'm working on the most recent one—the Junior G killing. Him and Black Hat."

I drew a blank. A complete blank. "What's the Black Hat—a club?"

"Black Hat was a who, not a what. Junior G was a major player

in the hip-hop world. And that kid who called himself Black
Hat was not much more than a gofer or some kind of bodyguard.
But he couldn't even guard himself. He was just a youngster
trying to get a career started, like a thousand other kids. He was
collateral damage. They got hit while they were in the back seat
of Junior's chauffeured wheels, just as they was leaving a parking
garage."

"Oh. So how many other carcasses have there been?"

"Six."

I had more or less been living in a cave the last months, deep
into the booze-soaked depression. But even so, I didn't understand how I could have missed hearing about the mass murder of
six black children. "Jesus Christ! Six kids were murdered?"

"They didn't all get killed at the same time. And they weren't
all children. It's the so-called rap wars."

Blank. Again.

"Rap, fool," said Sweet. "R-A-P."

The light suddenly went on. "As in 'music,' you mean? That
kind of rap?"

"You ain't too dumb, are you?"

A dim memory of a news bulletin: a well-known rapper shot
to death as he rode in the back of a limo on Grand Central Park-
way. But that seemed like at least a year ago. I asked Sweet if that
was one of the victims.

"That was Phat Neck," he supplied. "He was one of the biggest names around."

"I see."

I guess I saw. Since I loathed rap music, the name of one of
its big stars meant nothing to me. Rap had been around long
enough to begin influencing every other kind of music. It had
seeped into virtually every aspect of life in the States. They sold
cars and diet cola with it. They used it to teach kids how to read

on educational TV. You never saw a movie anymore that didn't feature it. And now it had gone global. Yet it was no huge effort for me to tune it out. I managed to do so because I disliked and resented it, maybe even feared it, because to my ears it was so rude and simplistic, and so very pleased with itself.

"And who were the others killed? I mean, other than this young boy Black Hat?"

"It started with Rawhide. Busta Jelly was next. Then Daddy Million. On and on, like I said. Big names in the industry."

The industry, eh? Leman was getting all Hollywood hincty. It sounded as if he might actually have been a fan of one or all of the murdered stars. But you're a grown man, I wanted to shout. Don't you already know the kind of simplistic stuff they say in those songs?

"One after the other," Sweet said. "They all been hit one after the other. Riding in cars or walking out of after-hours clubs or hotels. It looks like the same kind of turf war that killed Tupac in Vegas. A 'rap war,' like the papers call it. The Department couldn't care less as long as no 'civilians'—nobody white—get hurt. Let the niggers kill each other over some stupid record label design . . . or copyrights . . . or women . . . or crack . . . or whatever the fuck the argument is.

"But a group of black officers started a stink about it. We don't care what these guys say about the police in their songs. Shit, they got just as much right as anybody else to criticize the police. Just as much right to live. And just as much right after they're dead to have the killer caught and punished.

"I guess the brass got tired of us squawking about the whole thing. They put me on this special unit that works out of Twelfth Street. It's been six months now and we're getting nowhere, still looking up our own asses. Black people in this city have had it up to here with these killings and now a lot of groups are demanding action. That's too bad about your friend, but I gotta go along with Loveless on it. She was just unlucky—the way Black Hat was just unlucky. Maybe you oughta sue that stupid doll."

Leman Sweet, fighter for justice. I sat back, thinking it over. My goodness, life did still hold a few surprises. The situation held echoes of my encounter with Frank Loveless, the Bad Lieutenant. In both cases there was a cop who thought a lot of himself, a cop I didn't like or trust, but neither of them was anybody's fool. And I was damned if I could find any holes in their more than reasoned arguments.

Little Nan was not happy.

A nasty ploy presented itself to me then. Underhanded. Gender-based bullshit.

The notorious mantrap Aubrey Davis, my best friend, had helped take a little heat off of me back when Sweet's partner was killed and Sweet was making my life a misery. Leman had a pitiable jones for her and had in general made an idiot of himself. Not entirely his fault. Aubrey had that effect on guys and knew how to work it to full advantage.

"All right," I said with a sigh. "What you say makes sense. But if you find you have a minute to give to the Ida Williams thing, would you give me a call?"

I hastily scribbled a phone number on an edge of the paper tablecloth and tore it off. "I'll be spending a lot of time at my friend Aubrey's apartment. You might recall meeting her—tall? kind of nice looking? See, Aubrey's a real collector of these dolls. She must've bought eight or nine of them from Ida in the past and she's so upset over what happened that she doesn't like to be alone at night."

"This," he said slowly, looking down at the paper, "is Aubrey's number?"

"Um-hum."

Oh yeah. I'm going to feminist hell.

CHAPTER 6

LET ME OFF UPTOWN

I LOOKED DOWN BALEFULLY at Dilsey and Mama Lou lying among the discarded Kleenex and junk mail in the wicker trash basket. I shook my head. Should I throw them away now, once and for all?

I reached for them, but then withdrew my hand. Might as well wait until the basket was full. Then I'd just toss everything, including those traitors, into a garbage bag and consign it to the big can downstairs.

I dressed in the gender-neutral downtown uniform: black jeans, black shirt, black ankle boots, long leather jacket. I was going for hyper-low profile. I met my father for lunch once dressed like this and he had asked me in all earnestness what had happened in my life to make me want to look like Johnny Cash. I gave a minute's thought to wearing a tie, but then decided against it; it would probably just call more attention to those natural resources on my chest.

Sure, I wanted to make a few dollars, but that wasn't the chief reason for hitting the street that day. I planned to set up shop at

Fifteenth and Broadway, Ida's old corner—just hang over there and talk to some of the other street vendors. I figured one of them must have at least known where she lived. It also occurred to me that if her fellow buskers were as out of touch with the news as I tend to be, they might not even be aware that she was dead.

It was a market day, so there were hundreds of people about. Before opening my case, I wandered from one vendor's table to the other, looking lazily over their wares and chatting with any of them who felt like it. Even the Nigerian fellow with the musk.

I played a couple of numbers, starting with "Blue Gardenia," which was one of my solos with Hank and Roamer. A few customers leaving the nearby electronics store stopped to listen and dropped a couple of dollars into my case. I did "Gone with the Wind" and "Street of Dreams," then knocked off for a few minutes to drink a cup of hot cider I purchased in the market.

There was an older white guy who sold sunglasses, decent looking but flimsy knockoffs of the designer brands.

An Asian guy who was displaying silver bracelets and rings.

An attractive black woman in her forties with a stack of hand-knitted wool hats.

I talked to them all during the morning and afternoon. None of them had had more than a nodding acquaintance with Ida.

The day wore on and I continued to play periodically. "What's New," "Just Friends," "Prelude to a Kiss," and a few requests, including one from a white lady with infant twins in a double stroller, who asked for "On the Street Where You Live" and then didn't give me penny one.

Around four o'clock, however, there was a kind of shift change and a new group of vendors replaced most of the earlier ones.

Two college-age boys hawking the paperbound screenplays for old and new movies.

A gregarious old Irishman with ropes of fake pearls, three for five dollars—I indulged in a trio of those.

A tall well-built brother about thirty-five, who sold coffee-table art books at wildly discounted prices. Upon arrival, he pulled out a boom box and began loading it with a Clifford Brown tape. I'd seen the guy before, I realized, plying his trade a little farther uptown. It was summertime, if I remember right, and I'd looked his way twice owing to that torso of his, in a white fishnet undershirt. My interest now was strictly academic. Maybe the long bout of depression had sapped all my sexual energy. I just didn't much care.

It was not until I tipped an imaginary hat to him that he noticed I was standing there, set up to provide live entertainment. He smiled and punched the machine off. I played "Imagination" while he waited on a couple of people, and after I did "Out of this World" he applauded.

"You're not bad," he said, walking up close. From his slow appraisal of me, boots to eyebrows, I gathered he was referring both to the sounds and the girl making them.

On automatic pilot, I gave him that appreciative look right back.

"You come around here a lot?"

"No," I said. "What about you?"

"Two, three days a week."

"You know, I see a lot of books for sale on the street these days. New books. You've got a fabulous selection of stuff here at less than half the price of the bookstore. I was just wondering, how can you sell them so cheap? I mean, where do you get them from—a wholesaler?"

His only answer was one little smile.

"What about some coffee? A little lunch?" he said.

"Some other time. I have another nosy question for you." I stopped him from speaking by holding up my hand. "Not about your business," I assured him. "It's about the older woman who sells the dolls. You know who I mean?"

"Yeah. What about her?"

"Have you seen her lately?"

He thought about it for a moment. "No. We've had different schedules the last couple of weeks."

"I was hoping to buy a couple of her dolls for my nieces. You have any idea where she lives?"

Again, the mysterious smile.

"What? Why are you looking at me like that?"

"I was just wondering," he said in a remarkable imitation of my voice, subtly distorted with coyness, "where do you get that *fabulous* selection of bullshit?" He fluttered his bony hands girlishly in front of his face.

I am a sucker for long fingers on a man. Have I mentioned that?

I joined in his mocking laughter; I couldn't help it. "Okay," I said, "you got me. How'd you know it was bullshit?"

"Malik," he said, indicating the incense man. "He said the police were asking questions about Ida—because she had been killed. He told them he didn't know anything. I wasn't here when they came around."

"Does he know anything?"

"I don't think so."

"And you—do you know anything? Specifically, where she lived."

"Why are you really asking?"

"Because." Boy, my witty repartee was awesome. "Because I'm trying to do right by her."

"Little late for that. She's dead."

"Trust me, I'm not just messing around. I've got a good reason for wanting to know . . . What? Now what are you looking at?"

"What should I call you?"

"Nan."

"When can I call you?"

"Oh, pish."

"You're gorgeous, Nan. But I guess you get that a lot."

I let that lame stuff pass. "Well, do you?" I insisted.

"Do I what, Shorty?"

"Know where she lived."

He then nodded ever so slightly at a dented taupe-colored station wagon parked at the meter across the way. "Ida had her sewing machine fixed once. I picked it up from the shop and brought it to her place."

"Where was that?"

"Up on Amsterdam."

"Remember the exact address?"

"If I think real hard, I might."

That grin of his was making me feel like Little Red Riding Hood.

Come on, nitwit. What would Aubrey say now? I didn't know! But then, Aubrey would never be questioning a man about a murdered woman's address.

I did the best I could: "Hmm . . . What can I do to get you thinking hard?"

He gave up the address.

"Are you sure that's where she lived? Because there is no Ida Williams at that address in the phone book. I've looked."

"I swear," he said, "that's it."

I took my ballpoint out of my shirt pocket.

"How about dinner. Instead of lunch."

"Done. Tell me why she's not in the book."

"When I delivered the sewing machine, the name on the bell wasn't Williams. It was Rose. Alice Rose. I figured Ida lived with a friend or maybe she was a sublet."

"Excellent," I said, writing the name and street address down.

"You like spicy food?"

"Not at all," I said. "I'll call you." I handed him the pen and paper so that he could write down his name and number.

He handed them back. "Howard? You do *not* look like a Howard."

"I OWE YOU BIG-TIME, J."

"That's okay, Smash-up. There's nothing I like better than calling in favors. And this gumball owes me big-time."

Justin and I stood just outside a cavernous no-name bar on Amsterdam. Foreign territory to me. I knew Manhattan below Thirty-fourth Street like the back of my hand. I knew parts of Harlem—fellow musicians' apartments, the Studio Museum, a couple of bars, and of course the faded glory of Sugar Hill, where Aubrey had once lived in a glamorous sublet. I even had some familiarity with a few neighborhoods in Brooklyn. But the Upper West Side—north of Lincoln Center and south of Harlem—was not my beat.

J and I were waiting for Lefty. Not that that was the gumball's name. I didn't know the gumball's name yet. Only that he was one of many less-than-upright characters from Justin's world—and Aubrey's world, if one is to be honest about it. Low-level leg breakers and coke dealers, strip club employees, fixers, bartenders who also acted in porn movies or ripped off warehouses in their spare time. Lefty was from that world.

He drove a damn pretty car, though. Pulled up in it a few minutes after we arrived.

"You're sure this guy knows what it is you want him to do?" I asked as we watched the driver approach.

"Oh yeah."

"That favor he owes you must be a motherfucker."

"A little matter of an alibi. Let's just say it made about twenty-five years' worth of difference in his life, and leave it at that."

"I'm leaving it even as we speak."

"You can pay me back, too, Smash-up. And you don't have to break no laws to do it."

"Anything."

"My boyfriend, Kenny, wants to take us to lunch—a crab cakes and champagne blowout."

"That's all I have to do?"

"That's all. Favor repaid."

"I'm there, buddy."

Once he got up close, Lefty wasn't such a bad-looking white guy—not a gorilla at all. The ponytail was a mistake, but not, as it was with some men, a capital offense. He was on the short side; Justin and I both towered over him.

Lefty wasn't very polite to Justin. His jaw tight, he nodded perfunctorily at him and refused to meet his eyes while Justin was reciting Ida's address.

"Got it," he muttered. "Let's go."

"Just a minute, you rude thing!" Justin ribbed him. "There's a lady present. This is my friend Thelma. Thelma, this is, uh, Mark."

"Mark" may or may not have been Lefty's real name. But Thelma as an alias for me? Puh-leeeze. Thanks a lot, Justin.

Mark barely looked at me, obviously eager to be somewhere else. But then, when he finally turned his eyes in my direction he did a double take.

I could see him seeing me writhing up there on that stage under all the blue and orange lightbulbs.

"Nice to meet you, Thelma. You work at Caesar's?"

"No," I said, "but I'm thinking about auditioning. I've got an act with a live chicken."

"Really? Great . . . great." Lost in a reverie, he was. Fixated on my chest. There is something about short guys and tits.

"So you think I've got a shot at being hired, Mark?" I asked.

"Great . . . great . . ."

I think he might have been content to stand there staring all afternoon, that private movie going on in his head.

"Okay, children. Enough foreplay," Justin announced. "Let's do it."

J and I left first. We quickly located Ida's building, a good-looking white stone affair with a pillared entrance, and went into the lobby.

No Johnny Cash drag for me that day. I wore a brown wool mini and a crocheted top under a sweater coat, a cashmere beret, a nice pair of heels, and carefully applied makeup. Method act-ing. Who was I? Assistant to an ad agency honcho. Partner in a successful independent film distribution company. Girlfriend of a prominent European art dealer. Any of those would fly if I found myself face-to-face with a building super or a curious neighbor. I'd explain that I was so desperate to find an apartment that I was going house to house.

I checked out the buzzer setup. My friend from Union Square had given me righteous information. No Ida Williams in the building, but in apartment 6C, Alice Rose.

Our breast man bustled into the lobby a few minutes later. I saw him reach into his back pocket and withdraw a shiny, thin instrument. He had us through the inner door in no time.

J and I took the elevator to the sixth floor and scoped out 6C. Lefty came up the stairs then, noiseless as a shadow, and Justin signaled him from down the hall.

I was dispatched to play lookout near the elevator. And it was not until I heard the thing whirring inside its cage, lowering itself to the lobby, that it occurred to me to be petrified.

Some of the old folks in my family used to call me the Bulldog. That was because once I got an idea in my head, I was unstoppable: demonstrating to my parents why I had to have an expensive fountain pen, convincing them to let me go to Europe—whatever. So it was with digging deeper into Ida's murder. I was helping two men break into an apartment. Of course we weren't going to rob the place, but we were breaking and entering. A crime any way you sliced it.

I began to sweat profusely, imagining that the super had watched us enter on a security monitor and was at that moment on his way up with the police.

I heard a dull pop from the area where Lefty was working and my heart popped along with it. The elevator was on the way back up now. Where would it stop? Where it stops, nobody knows. What was that from—spin the bottle?

It stopped at the fifth floor. Just below me. I heard voices down there—a man and a woman talking amiably about their respective Thanksgiving Day plans—and then they trailed off.

A hand suddenly around my waist, and a gruffly whispered "Okay, Thelma."

I almost jumped out of my $98 Ecco pumps.

"Just let me know if they give you any trouble at Caesar's," Lefty said. "Maybe you and me'll have a drink next time I'm by there."

He didn't wait for my answer. By the time I recovered my voice, he was halfway down the stairs.

Ida's apartment was something of a surprise. I guess I had expected a small place with secondhand furniture, littered with remnants of the cheap fabrics she used to make the dolls. A few shelves groaning with dusty knickknacks and a family Bible—or possibly a witches' handbook. Some humble canned goods in the kitchen. Maybe a mangy half-starved cat.

Not at all. The large living room was airy, clean, and unfcluttered. An armoire in one corner of the room held twenty or thirty of her dolls. There was a nice kitchen, spotless, with all the amenities, including a post-modern refrigerator of gleaming stainless steel.

The walk-in closet in her sparse bedroom was neatly organized and, besides the predictable assortment of sweaters, raincoat, pants, skirts, and so on, held no fewer than three gorgeous frocks every bit as tasteful as the one she was wearing the night she died. Her sewing machine was in there, too, on a roll-away table. At the foot of the queen-size bed was a plaid mohair throw to die for.

I had only one question: When could I move in?

"Not too shabby," I commented to Justin, who was sitting contentedly on the Shaker-style bench in front of the largest of the front room windows.

"Girl, you said it."

"We'd better get a move on, J. Let's start searching this place."

He threw his head back and shook out imaginary tresses. "Just imagine it! I'm on a dangerous mission to find ze formula before ze Germans get it. I feel like Hedy Lamarr!"

"Let's start with the boxes in the bedroom closet, Miss Lamarr."

Those proved to contain nothing more than her summer clothes carefully packed in cedar chips. Being as quiet as possible, we opened the bureau drawers, felt around in the folds of the sofa and chairs, checked out the shelves of the linen closet, pulled the things out of the bathroom cabinet. It was a catch-as-catch-can search, because we didn't really know what we were looking for. Then, in a hatbox in the hall closet, I found something—a wad of money. About eight hundred bucks.

"What do you think? Not just pin money?" Justin said.

"Not just pin money," I repeated. "It's a lot of cash to have in the house, but not enough to mean anything in particular. Maybe this is everything she earned the last few months. Maybe she didn't like banks. A lot of older people don't."

We continued to poke into things here and there.

"So who do you think this Alice Rose person is?" he asked.

"That's what I'm wondering. Not a roommate, obviously. This is a one-person household. Ida must have been subletting, like that guy from the farmers market said. Probably an illegal sublet."

"May be," he answered. "But even if it is, how could she afford it? This is kind of a fabulous building."

"Hmm. I agree. Still—Alice Rose might be rent-controlled. Maybe she's one of those lucky people who's been living here forever and is still paying two hundred a month or something."

I noticed that he had stopped rifling through the bedside table and was now staring at a photograph in a gold frame.

"What are you looking at?"

"I found this way up high on the bookshelf," he said. "Look at my girl Ida. She's a real glamour puss in this picture."

I went over to the bookcase. "Let's see."

Ida was twenty-five or thirty years younger in the photograph, which seemed to be a professionally done portrait. She was wearing a white gown with a beaded bodice. "Holy mackerel. Glamour puss is right. I've got an old Sarah Vaughan album where she's dressed just like this."

"Look at her makeup. Whitney Houston must've seen this picture somewhere."

"Weird, isn't it?" I said. "Now I'm wondering how she went from *this* to peddling voodoo dolls on the street. Keep looking, J."

We never found a secret formula, or a bankbook showing half a million dollars, or even a rent receipt with Alice Rose's name on it. But, just as we were about to give up and leave the place, I went over to slide the closet door closed. I had seen the huge wicker basket in there containing her sewing things. On a hunch, I went back to it and dug my hand deep inside.

I felt something at the bottom of the basket. When I brought it out, I could see it was an old manila folder. I plunged my hand in again and came up with an object much larger and more solid—more like a scrapbook.

I opened the folder first. "Look, Justin. Another glam photo of Ida when she was young."

"Great dress! She looks like Della Reese before the lard took over. If those earrings are still in this house, I'm sorry but they are mine."

He grabbed the folder to get a closer look, and a patch of yellowing newspaper fell out. Pictured were Ida and a dashing black man in tails, their straightened hair gleaming like a model's mouth in a tooth whitener ad. Justin and I began to laugh hysterically, until I remembered where we were and quieted him down.

"Miller (left) and Priest," the caption read. I checked the top of the page, which was torn. All that remained was the word "Cleveland."

"This says her last name is Priest, right?" J asked. "I thought it was Williams."

I shrugged.

The only other photo in there was a two-head shot of the same duo, taken, probably, ten years after the first shot.

I passed the photo over to Justin. "They're something, aren't they?" I said. "What do you think the story is? Why were they in the newspaper? Did they win the Irish Sweepstakes or something? Doesn't look like a wedding announcement. Looks more like they were in show business—as if that newspaper thing was an ad. Like this guy and Ida had an act—partners. Something like that. What do you think they did—tap-dance?"

Justin shook his head.

"We'd better get out of here," I said. "Let's just see what's in this book I—"

"What? What is it?"

It took a minute for me to answer because I was still trying, as my friends in therapy say, to process it.

"It's a yearbook," I finally said, softly. "A high school yearbook."

"What—from 1920?"

"No. Later than that. Ninety-six."

Justin took it from my hands. "Stephens Academy, 1996," he read. And then he shrugged. "I don't get it."

"Neither do I," I said. "That's my father's school. He's the principal."

CHAPTER 7

FINE BROWN FRAME

I LOOKED OUT at the trees, as I had been doing for the last twenty minutes, the yearbook pressed tightly against me.

The majestic view of Central Park from Aubrey's windows had always been my favorite thing about her apartment, and now I was drinking that view in, lost in thought, lost in the trees.

Aubrey came out of the bathroom wearing a towel. Around her head, that is. That was all she wore.

She sat down on the mile-long sectional—did people who live in high-rises ever buy any other kind of couch?—and began to lacquer her toenails.

She had phoned me earlier in the day to tell me that Leman Sweet, whose sweet tooth for her was no secret, had taken the bait. He'd called Aubrey, said he wanted to meet with me and knew I was staying at her place. It would be convenient, he said, to drop by there tonight on his way home.

"Home—in whatever cave that might be," Aubrey had scoffed. She had had her fun taunting him in the past, leading him on, but she had never forgotten nor forgiven my rough treatment at his hands.

Luckily I had not yet taken the trash out at my own home. I remembered telling Sweet how it was really Aubrey, not me, who had a thing for Ida Williams's dolls. So before heading uptown, I plucked the two little hoodoo queens out of the wastebasket beneath my desk and threw them in my knapsack. They now stood on the windowsill, facing out, possibly enjoying the park view as much as I was.

Aubrey had commented while I was positioning them, "Be sure you take those old raggedy-ass dolls outta here when you leave tonight."

"Don't worry," I said. "They don't stay where they're not wanted."

"So what do you think it means?" she asked.

"What? Leman? I have no idea what he's going to say tonight."

"Not that, fool. I mean the book. From where your father works. What was it doing in that woman's apartment?"

"No idea."

I had been in the grip of inchoate fear ever since I laid eyes on the thing. No clue why Ida would have had it. There was probably a very sensible explanation—she had some smart-as-a-whip grandchild, or niece or nephew, who attended that brat academy, and the fact that my father ran the place was sheer coincidence. That much wasn't so hard to swallow. But why was the thing at the bottom of her sewing basket? Hidden. That had to mean something.

I had not only broken into Ida Williams's apartment, I had removed what might turn out to be evidence from it. Before Justin and I closed up the place, I grabbed the yearbook. I had no idea at all how my father fit into things; I just knew I couldn't leave that book in the apartment. I had my problems with Daddy, but the old blood tie was still there.

No blood ties with Ida. But that didn't stop me from stuffing the most recent photograph of her and—what should I call him—Mr. Miller, her would-be stage partner, inside the book's back cover and taking that, too.

When it all came out, Leman Sweet was going to crucify me unless someone stayed his hand. I looked over at Aubrey's perfect frame. Lord, I was pimping my best friend.

"You remember I told you once about reading a story in the newspaper, Aubrey? While I was in Paris. Remember, I said I read about a woman getting murdered. I had never heard of her or anybody involved in the killing—but somehow I knew she was going to have some kind of connection to my life."

"Yeah, and she did. In the worst kind of way."

"Right. Well, that's what it felt like when I saw the yearbook. As if my pop was part of this thing with Ida. Or part of those fucking dolls—or something. I mean, those two things—a high school yearbook and an old folder with a couple of photos and a newspaper ad—they were together in the basket. And, I don't know—I just don't know. But it freaked me out."

"You starting to sound as stupid as Justin. He's always crossing his toes or wearing some special ring for good luck or some other foolishness. Ask me, you both crazy."

I shrugged, embarrassed, unable to mount a counterargument. It still amazed me how easily I had bought into the whole myth of the dolls and their special powers, as Ida had put it. I had never thought of myself as particularly superstitious. A believer in fate, yes. But not a slave to superstition.

Aubrey went in to dress then. I had time to ponder the other question of the night: What was Leman going to tell me? I was betting that the police had by now identified Ida, and probably found out where she lived. A shiver went through me at the thought that Justin and I might have been caught in that apartment, that the cops might have arrived at her place, realized that someone was inside, and announced themselves in their own special way—with guns blazing.

The intercom buzzer sounded.

Aubrey called from her bedroom at the far end of the hall, "That's gotta be Numb Nuts. Get it, Nan, will you?"

I did. "Sergeant Sweet to see you," the doorman announced.

"Let him up," I responded.

Yeah, let him up. Showtime.

"Hiya, Leman," I greeted him.

He nodded at me, friendly enough. I guess I was getting away with calling him by his so-called Christian name.

"Y'all ain't busy, are you?" he asked, scanning the room.

"No problem."

I led him into the living room and saw him to a seat. I stood there, not speaking, while he continued to look for signs of Aubrey.

A few seconds later she appeared. Long legs in white tights. Yellow angora sweater that bared one shoulder. Tresses tousled here, pinned up there. She made that all-important eye contact with Sweet, the look that promised—lied—so much.

"Hey," she said simply, making that a word of at least three syllables.

"You remember my friend Aubrey, don't you, Leman?"

Poor Numb Nuts. He began to laugh idiotically, trying not to stutter. Finally he managed a "How you doing, Aubrey?"

"I'm good." Long pause, sly grin, eye contact unbroken. "Nanette, did you offer Sweet something to drink?"

"Something to drink, Leman?"

"Naw, that's okay," he answered quickly, not even pretending to look at me.

"It is *not* okay," Aubrey said. "I'm gonna get you a beer. I got a Heineken in there with your name on it. How would you like that, Sweet?"

He nodded so vigorously I thought he might break his neck.

"So," I said, taking the chair across from him, "something's happened?"

"What happened?"

"I don't know. I thought you were going to tell me."

"Oh. Yeah. Something did happen. I called Loveless about that old lady you been talking about. They didn't find any papers on her, like you told me. But they finally ID'd her from prints. Ida Williams was not her real name."

"Uh-huh."

"More like it, you could say it was only one of her names. She had four or five . . ."

Aubrey came in with the beer then. She placed it on the glass table along with a stein and then demurely withdrew from the room.

". . . four or five aliases and a record going back forty years."

"You're kidding." An automatic response from me. I knew, suddenly, clearly, that he wasn't.

"She did a couple of stretches for forgery, grand larceny—like that," he added.

It was my turn to laugh idiotically. For the same reason he had done it: I could not find my tongue.

Leman twisted his head around. Aubrey was on the kitchen telephone and he was straining to hear what she was saying. But she remained tantalizingly out of reach, her voice a distant purr.

"Looks like that old lady wasn't 'xactly what you thought she was," he said. Then he took a long drink of beer and wiped at his mouth with the pink paper napkin our hostess had provided.

"Looks that way," I said slowly, thinking.

"Why don't we tell Aubrey about it, too."

"Hmm. Good idea," I murmured. "We'll tell her in a minute."

I was thinking, quite frankly, Will I catch more hell if I tell him now or later? Can I get away with saying nothing at all about my foray into housebreaking? I looked over at the year-book, which lay facedown next to the dolls. Aubrey's siren act was my salvation. But would her protection extend to my father if indeed it turned out that he had something to do with Ida's misdeeds—let alone with her death? No way.

I recalled how much Leman resented me, when first we met, for what he saw as my know-it-all "college girl" airs. If my over-achieving father had done anything wrong, he'd take more heat than a common criminal off the street. Leman would see to it. That chubby-cheek Negro on the Supreme Court had coined the phrase that seemed to apply here: there would be a high-tech lynching.

"How about some pretzels, Sweet?" That was Aubrey calling from the kitchen.

"Yeah, how about some?" I prompted him, still scheming, putting off the inevitable.

"Naw. I'm watching my salt," he answered.

"Good for you," Aubrey said, appearing for a moment in the doorway. She quickly disappeared.

"I still don't think anybody paid to have that woman killed," he told me then. "The fact she had a record don't prove a thing. This is America—anybody black could have a record. But the best thing you and Aubrey could do is stay out of this Ida Williams business."

He chuckled maliciously. "You kinda got up Loveless's nose the other night, you know. He sounds like he's a little pissed anyway 'cause of Ida's record and stuff. The case maybe ain't as simple as he thought. Anyway, you don't want him bringing down no kinda heat on you. Believe me."

A little mouse squeak escaped involuntarily from my chest.

"What's the matter?"

I pushed down the second bout of idiotic laughter. "Look, Leman. I—I better tell you something."

He waited for me to go on. I watched his face slowly turn to stone.

I got up and retrieved the yearbook. Little by little, in the course of recounting how I spent my Thursday afternoon, I confessed to unlawful entry, tampering with evidence, and God knows what other lesser included offenses, as the parlance would have it. Told him all about Ida's show business partner, too. And the wad of money in the hatbox.

"God*damn*! Same old Cueball. Why didn't they drown you at birth?" He gestured at the yearbook. "Give that to me, girl, before I—"

"How we doing in there?" Aubrey's bright voice broke the rope of tension in the room.

"I'll let Leman answer that one," I said. "Come on in, Aubrey. And I'll take one of those beers, too."

Leman snatched the photograph out of the book, looked at it contemptuously, and tossed it aside. He was furiously turning the pages of the yearbook as he went back to strafing me. "What kind of stupid Cueball idea made you do that shit in the first place? Are you crazy, woman? Or you just determined to drive me crazy? And why the hell would you think your daddy's got anything to do with anything? That's just plain dumb."

My face was burning. It looked as though, once again, I was taking the superstition stuff much too seriously, seeing ill omens where there were none.

"Look what I got for you, Sweet."

Aubrey was holding a large plate brimming with snack crackers, looking like a kind of lascivious Welcome Wagon lady. "All low-salt."

Leman began to speak, but she had already smeared one of the biscuits with softened cheese and was popping it into his mouth with newly manicured fingers.

She sat near him on the sofa. "Don't let me interrupt," she said. "Go ahead."

He cleared his throat.

I sighed, resigned. "Yes, go on, Sergeant Sweet. Where were we?"

But he did not resume his harangue. Instead, he asked, "What's the name of this school again?"

"Stephens Academy," I answered, needlessly, because he suddenly turned back to the front cover, keeping his place in the book with the other hand.

"This is the graduating class of ninety-six, right?"

"Yeah, why?"

I got up to see what was so interesting. He was looking down at a pretty young girl in cap and gown, a winningly crooked smile on her face. Her face was not so much pretty as arresting, full of dramatic planes, the perfect setting for her huge almond-shaped eyes and full mouth.

"I'm through yelling at you, Cueball."

"You are?"

"Yeah. I am. You just gave me an idea. Shit, I'll even let you call me by my first name."

"See?" said Aubrey, pleased as all get out, as if she had just solved all our problems—as if she even knew what he meant.

"No, I don't see," I said. "What idea did I give you, Leman?"

"Never mind that for the moment. You know what I told you about my assignment over on Twelfth Street."

"Homicide unit. Dead kid. Rap music stars."

"That's right. You see this little girl here? She was going with the last one to die—Kevin Benson, aka Black Hat. He and this little girl—Felice Sanders—were supposed to be married."

Connection! I let out a big breath. Was this what the karmic synchronicity was all about? Not my father but some kid at his school?

But wait a minute. So what? This girl went to Stephens. What did that have to do with anything?

I asked Leman the same question. "So this rap kid had a little white girlfriend who went to my father's school. What difference does it make? You don't think she killed him, do you?"

"Of course not. From what I been able to gather, she was crazy about him."

"And besides, she's not at the school anymore. She already graduated, right?"

"Right. I had no idea where she went to school before now. It had no bearing on anything. But I decided yesterday to interview her again, tie up some loose ends."

He seemed to hesitate there.

"And?" I said.

"The thing is, in the time since I last talked to her, she ran away from home—or at least that's how her mother put it. The point is, we can't locate her now."

"Oh."

"Now, since you found this yearbook, it brings me to another way you can help me out."

"Oh?"

"Yeah. And in exchange I'll keep in touch with Loveless—see what's happening with the Ida Williams case. And keep him from eating you alive."

"You want me to go to Stephens and talk to my father about Felice."

"You got it, Cue. See what kind of dope you can get me on her. Did she hang with a particular group? Is there somebody she might have stayed friends with, moved in with? Stuff like that. We got limited manpower at the Twelfth Street squad. We're looking for the girl, but we got a thousand other things to do.

But you, you got an in there at the school, see, what with your
father being the chief. It may be a waste of time, I don't know.
Just nose around a little bit, which oughta be second nature to
you."

Better to waste your time than mine. That's what he was saying. But I pretended not to recognize it. I needed the pipeline to
the Ida Williams investigation that only he could provide. And
I sure as hell didn't want Loveless to eat me alive.

CHAPTER 8

IT'S EASY TO REMEMBER

I REMEMBER WRITING a poem once and showing it, at my mother's urging, to my pop. I must have been nine or ten.

He was impressed by the fact of it—and told me as much—but he had to be honest, it wasn't very good. *However*, he added, that wasn't the important thing. The important thing was, he knew I was capable of better.

For the next three weeks, whenever he came home from work he'd have a different library book for me—the Langston Hughes reader, collected Emily Dickinson, a little leather-bound edition of Jean Toomer's *Cane*, etc.

I never touched one of those damn books. And I was nineteen before I tried to write another poem.

My pop is kind of a stick.

He was an excellent provider. Tireless. Upstanding. Rational. Fair. Generous even—I mean, it was Pop who paid to have my friend Aubrey's appendix removed; her own mother was at a poker tournament in Jersey when Aubrey collapsed. So, I'd have to concede that he usually means well, but he is an unregenerate stick.

Making my peace with that—without benefit of a shrink—has been a pretty long haul. It did not help matters that in the middle of the process, he left my mother in order to marry a white woman some twenty years younger.

He and I have been circling each other warily ever since. We speak periodically, sit together at family funerals, exchange birthday gifts (his to me is invariably a big fat practical check), and at Christmastime he takes me to a grand dinner somewhere. Thank the baby Jesus, he decided his child-siring days were behind him, so there are no half siblings for me to deal with.

It felt as though we'd go on like that forever, the relationship attenuating inch by inch as the years went on, until he died. But last spring changed that shit.

The violent death of his sister, my aunt Vivian, sent the thing between Pop and me spiraling off in a whole other direction. As if we needed anything else laying there between us, anything else to regret, too hot to handle, too tangled up and painful to talk about. And so Vivian's awful death and my failure to prevent it was now something else to be trotted off to the boneyard and buried.

I was watching my father, but he didn't know it. He was waiting at the traffic light on Hudson Street, that familiar look on his face. When he got that checked-out expression on his face, it wasn't because he was distracted. Far from it, he was thinking up a storm, and almost always about Stephens Academy and what could be done to make it an even finer place. Daddy is a great believer in "planning ahead." I'm kind of not, to his disappointment.

He had just had his lunch, no doubt, and was taking the air before returning to his office at the school. Stephens Academy—a low-rise building on the western fringe of Greenwich Village—

had no beautifully landscaped grounds or grassy commons. But there was a well-kept patch of green behind the iron gates that fronted the street, and at the back of the school, away from the traffic, the lawn fanned out prettily. There were a few picnic tables back there where the students took their lunch on nice days, the flower and herb garden where the botany classes were often held, and a small stone cottage in the Japanese style—for poetry readings? bamboo flute recitals? teenage meditation?

I stood inside the gate watching him come closer and closer in his deep-green overcoat. Burberry's. I knew, because when we had our Christmas get-together last year, his Mrs. had just presented it to him. He wore no hat and I could see the nice ripple of gray growing in at his temple. Funny, I never noticed before, but I have his forehead. His mouth, too. I'm not a stick. But I am his. I'm his child.

Would he notice me?

Nope. He kept walking.

"Hey, Pop."

He stopped abruptly, just inside the gate, wheeled.

"Nanette. There's my daughter."

We embraced for a minute and then he held me away from him, taking me in. "You're looking well, daughter—nice and trim. Now, to what do I owe the pleasure? I used to try to get you to visit the school—"

I cut him off. "Shouldn't we go inside?"

I had hold of his arm, but he would not be moved. "Is something wrong?"

"No. I'm okay. And so is Mom."

He nodded. "All right. Let's go in."

Introduction to his faithful secretary. Not the faithful secretary I had met years ago. This one was under forty, had a very hip haircut, and wore khakis with her DKNY turtleneck. But, as the old one had done, she stood and grasped my hand warmly in both of hers, in that "Oh, you must be little Nanette" sort of grip.

Inside his office, I recognized the pen holder I had given him one year, and the silver picture frame, which held a photo of him and a now-celebrated former student at some school event.

"Do you by any chance have the student yearbook for ninety-six, Daddy?"

"Our yearbook? Of course. Why?"

"I'd like to look at it for a minute. To show you something."

I flipped through the book until I found what I was looking for. He had no particular recollections of Felice Sanders, but did recall that she had been a scholarship student.

"Why are you interested in this young woman, Nanette? Is she a friend of yours?"

"Not really. It's not worth explaining now, Pop. I just need to know if you remember her . . . if you knew anything about her personal life or maybe heard from her since she graduated."

I could see his mind working. Of course he wanted to know more, of course felt entitled to ask more. But on the other hand, he was thinking, the child does have a history of some fairly scarifying behavior. She's managed to stay in one piece without my knowing too many of the particulars. Probably best not to open the door to something I'm going to regret having asked about.

It almost made me laugh to think what he'd say if he knew I owned a gun. I thought, too, of my mother's hatred of him, still white-hot after all these years. I had an image of her waiting behind that iron gate instead of me. It would have shaken that super-dignified bearing of his to see her there with my piece pointed at his heart. I blinked those thoughts away.

"We'd have Felice's home address in the records," he said. "And maybe a family income statement. Grades and such things. Will that help?"

"Whatever you have."

"Actually," he said, "there is someone around who'd know a bit more about what she was like."

"Who?"

"Dan. Dan Hinton. He teaches English and doubles as a kind of guidance counselor—not officially—we have a bona fide school counselor. But Dan does have a degree in psychology as well, and the children like him. He seems to know how to talk to them, bring them out."

Oh brother.

There was one at every school. A man or woman closer in age to the kids than the average faculty member. Always thought he or she was "in touch" with what adolescents really needed. Dressed too young for his age. Tried to keep up with the music the kids listened to—track the pop culture idols as well as the current drugs of choice—master the latest slang. Thought of him- or herself as an excellent listener. Sickening stuff.

I remained with my father for another fifteen minutes. Actually it didn't even take that long to exhaust our usual list of discussion topics—how was Aubrey; did I need any money; was I managing to save any money; did I still study music with Jeff; how many students did I have in my French class. And from my side: how were the renovations on the apartment going; read any good books lately; where were he and the Mrs. thinking about vacationing next summer.

I kissed my pop good-bye and promised to join him and the Mrs. one night at the opera. Which was about as likely to happen as his plan to come by my apartment one day so that I could make one of my "famous" upside-down cakes for him.

AS I WALKED up to the third floor, I amused myself with predictions about what Dan Hinton would look like. The gaunt and rumpled grad student look, or would he be a tad out of shape with a premature bald spot? Glasses or not? Nerd or phony charm boy?

I nearly collided with a skinny ash-blond kid, his pants riding dangerously low on his hips, who was turning out of the classroom. Just over his shoulder, I caught my first glimpse of Dan Hinton.

Aha. Well, he didn't wear glasses. But he was real ugly. That is, if you think the young Harry Belafonte was ugly. D'ya think Denzel's ugly? Brad Pitt? Dan Hinton was in that league.

How was he dressed? Who cared?

"Nanette, right?" He stood up, and exhibited those shoulders. "I'm not psychic," he said, in a gravelly voice from heaven. "I saw your photo at Eddie's apartment when he and Amy asked me to dinner once. Are you looking for him?"

Nobody called my father Eddie.

What? Who? Oh, that's right, I hadn't spoken a word yet. I realized I had been fantasizing a bit. Okay, Nan, pull it together, girl.

"My father, you mean. No. I've already seen him. He said you might be able to answer a few questions about a former student of yours. Felice Sanders. She graduated in ninety-six."

"Did something happen to Felice?"

"No. I mean, I don't really know. I just thought she might be able to help me track down a friend of mine—and hers—a mutual friend. But now I'm having trouble locating her as well."

He appeared to take in that addle-brained fib for what it was. "Uh-huh. Well, it doesn't surprise me that you're having trouble catching up with Felice."

"Why? Have you kept in touch with her?"

"Off and on. By the way, wouldn't you like to have a seat?" He pointed to one of the kidney-shaped desk-chair combinations.

"Thanks. Are you sure I'm not keeping you from your work?"

"That's okay. It can wait."

I sat down, crossed my legs. He watched me do it. "You were saying . . . about keeping in touch?"

"Yes. Felice does sort of keep in touch. When she was at Stephens, she wasn't technically my student. She needed somebody to talk to. Like a lot of kids. She never seemed to click with many of the other students."

"So she didn't have buddies that she always hung out with? Was there maybe another girl that Felice might be rooming with now?"

"I doubt that. The other students liked her well enough, I think. But she tended to keep to herself. She's a nice girl. Talented. She wants to be a dancer—or did. The last few times we spoke she was out of focus—all over the place. Depressed. Angry. Kind of lost."

"Over her boyfriend's death?"

"You know about that then."

"Not really. I just heard her boyfriend was killed."

"It just about did her in. She loved Black Hat."

"Did you know him, too?"

He shook his head. "No. I just knew she seemed to genuinely love him. She was a junior when they met, when they fell in love. It did wonders for Felice. She's an adopted kid. Troubled background. Her adoptive father died. One bad thing after another. But after she met this boy, her life seemed to open up. By the time she graduated, she was talking about marriage. I hate what happened, to both of those kids. It was stupid—wrong."

Was this the guidance counselor for the millennium, or what? Not only does he get you through the ordeal of high school, he keeps track of you for life.

"What did you mean," I asked, "when you said you weren't surprised that I couldn't locate her?"

"Well, without breaking any confidences, I'll just say that since Black Hat died she's been kind of out of control. She's not—not so resourceful. What I mean is, she's vulnerable now and doesn't make the best choices."

"Choices of men, you mean."

"That's right. And the last time we spoke she mentioned a man I don't like the sound of. Obviously he's much older than she is. Listen, like I said, I shouldn't be discussing her personal life with a stranger. No offense. I know you're Eddie's kid and you'll be discreet, but . . ."

"I understand. Privileged information."

"No, she's not my patient. She's—"

He stopped there. I wondered for a minute, maybe more than a minute, She's not my patient, she's . . . what?

The fortyish Hinton seemed too responsible, too smart to be a casual seducer of students. But perhaps, once Felice Sanders was no longer a student, there had been something between them. Would that be unethical of him? I didn't know. I did know with every fiber of my being that if I was eighteen and "lost" and had someone like Dan Hinton interested in me, had him to talk to, lean on, whatever, I'd be in his bed like a shot.

But what was it about this guy? Was it just that he was too good to be true? A strong, intelligent, drop-dead gorgeous black man with a steady job who likes and respects children. Looks more like a daytime soap star than an English teacher. So what was it?

Oh, I knew what it was—I didn't much like him. Pretty, oh yeah. But I didn't like him.

"By the way," he said, "I'd like to ask you something."

"Me? What?"

"You know that poem of yours—the translation—in *Transfer*?"

I must have turned green at the mention of that name. Oh Jesus. He knew about that?

About ten years ago I did have a poem accepted in a toney little art magazine with that name. For a hot minute I had been a celebrity on campus. My father must have kept his copy all these years, shown it to him during that dinner party. Yikes!

"What about it?" I asked.

"It was kinda crap. Do you still write?"

I burst into unbridled laughter. What *was* it about this guy? The bastard had insulted me and here I was cracking up. Okay, maybe I was being too hard on him.

Smooth as a milkshake, he was. Maybe the kids did think he was cool. Maybe he was.

"So that was the extent of your relationship with Felice?" I asked a minute later. "Dutch uncle—nothing else?"

"I didn't—I never—" he stumbled, "slept with Felice."

"That's okay, you could have said 'fucked.' I won't tell Daddy."

He grinned.

A silence fell then. And not an uncomfortable one. He turned his gaze fully on me and I didn't look away, not once. After a few moments of that, I saw him glance down at his watch.

I got to my feet quickly. "Thanks for your time."

"No problem. Look, I don't know much more about Felice than what I told you. Just that she didn't apply to college. She planned to marry Black Hat and thought she might continue with her dancing. Oh yeah, I once asked how her family looked at her marrying a black man, and she said she thought if there was going to be any trouble about that, it would come from his family, not hers. Does that help you? I mean, help you with whatever it is you're doing."

"I don't know yet," I said. "Maybe. But thanks anyway." I turned to leave.

"I liked the *end* of the poem."

"Please—you don't have to say that."

"I know. I'm not lying to you. I really liked the end. And I thought a little flattery couldn't hurt, when I . . . when I asked you—"

"What did you want to ask me?"

"Out."

WHAT WAS GOING ON? I thought as I walked across Ninth Street. What was happening here? My erotic stuff was in mothballs these days, that's how I wanted it. I wasn't up for anything romantic. But it seemed these days that I was spewing come-hither pheromones to men all over New York City, fine ones at that. Who was going to hit on me next—the butcher?

I CAUGHT UP with Leman at the pizza stand on University Place, just around the corner from the building where he was headquartered. He was busy and had to forgo the barbecue joint that day. It was three o'clock and he was just grabbing a quick bite.

I reported on my visit to Stephens while he demolished three slices with meatballs and peppers.

Red sauce glistened on his chin.

"What other kind of crap did this Hinton dude lay on you?"

"You don't buy what he told me?"

"You mean you do? Ain't it a little funny that a teacher would know so much about Felice's business? I wouldn't be surprised if that slick son of a bitch was getting his . . ." He broke off there. "You educated niggers," he said, chuckling. "Always think you know it all, and couldn't find a fly on horseshit."

That again. What old resentments was he stewing about now? What uppity little girl had shot him down in eighth grade? Us bougie niggers always had our way in life greased, while poor prole Leman Sweet had to fight for every break he got, right?

Of course I was assuming that old, not fresh resentments were plaguing him. Sweet surely had a thousand legitimate complaints about life as a black cop—a black man. But, outside of his anger over the rap murders, he had never spoken with me about them.

Leman Sweet was a tough nut to crack. Obviously a bright man. Obviously a sharp cop. But his assumptions about me and mine were infuriating, and his quicksilver temper—the violence in him—scared me. Besides, even if Aubrey's charms were working on him, and even if he'd decided I might be useful to him with the Felice Sanders thing, he and I were not destined to be buddies. Whatever it was he thought he saw in me, he plainly despised it.

I waited patiently for him to finish his nasty laugh and get to the point.

"I saw that little girl at Black Hat's funeral. Sure, she was upset. What would you expect? Her fiancé was dead. But she wasn't no more crazy or 'lost' than any other kid would be in her place. She was crying and wailing. So what? It was a funeral."

"Listen, Leman. You wanted me to check out Felice's history at the school and I did. Dan Hinton seems like he cares about her. If he says she's kind of a loose cannon, I would tend to believe him."

"Okay, Cue. I don't have time to argue about that." He finished the last of his soda in one amazing gulp. "Anyway, maybe this Hinton is onto something. Felice's mother still hasn't heard from her. And come to think of it, the girl did go off on Black Hat's mama and daddy that day."

"What day?"

"The day of the funeral. I was there. Wanted to see if any of the rappers who showed up might be suspects in the shooting."

"How did she go off?" I asked. "Over what?"

"She was blaming Jacob and Lenore Benson, Black Hat's parents, for his murder. Said if they had listened to him, respected him, it never would have happened."

"What did that mean?"

"How do I know? Nobody seemed to know what she was talk-ing about. She probably didn't know, either. She was screaming at them—stuff about how she was going to pay them back for dissing him. How she was going to get revenge on them."

Revenge. More needless havoc was wreaked in the name of getting even than anything else I could think of. And what did revenge mean in this case? I should think losing Kevin was enough of a revenge on the Bensons. Well, it had probably been an idle threat anyway.

"What about Ida?" I asked. "Does Loveless have anything new?"

"I put a call in to him this morning. Haven't heard back yet. So you just going to have to cool it till he calls me. Meantime, no more second-story jobs—understand? Or I'll throw your ass to the dogs."

"Yassuh!" I spat out.

Leman went back to work, without thanking me for my efforts, I might add. I forgot that slight soon enough, though. I had a number of other things to think about.

For one, I had a date with Dan Hinton. Okay, so I'm a whore.

CHAPTER 9

THE MORE I SEE YOU

WHAT WAS I—a Cosby kid? The night's appointment with the beautiful Mr. Hinton was taking up way too much space in my head.

So I went out early that morning and played on the street.

I did a bunch of fast, muscular, hard bop numbers—even some aggressive, head-banger kind of improvising. I made next to no money. But that was all right—I was just playing for the sake of playing. Playing for the practice. Trying to get myself centered. I just didn't want to be acting like a silly broad all excited over the prospect of a date with a cute man.

My copy of the photo with Ida and Miller was in the sax case. When I had exhausted my macho man repertoire, I jumped on the subway and went up to Ida's old West Side neighborhood. I bought a big carry-out container of coffee and hit the streets, showing the picture to some of the local merchants and any of her former neighbors who deigned to speak to me. A few neighborhood denizens were engaged in dog walking, grocery shopping, and the like, and I pushed the photo to them wherever I found them. With a little prompting from me, the shoe repair man said he recognized Ida from the photo, but he'd never set eyes on Miller.

I took a brisk walk through Central Park and emerged at Columbus Circle, where I got back on the BMT and headed downtown once more. In a few minutes I was back at Union Square Park, currently the hub of my life, it seemed.

The farmers market was lovely with winter flowers and exotic pears and apples and brown breads warm from the oven. I walked among the stalls and continued to flash the photo at the regulars. No one knew Miller.

Man. That guy must have been a genius at covering his tracks—and his ass. Maybe he and Ida had both done the crimes. But it was only Ida who'd done the time. Miller had no prison record.

I had a reunion with my greasy old boyfriend, as Ida had teasingly referred to him. The homeless old gent who cadged money from shoppers and ran errands for some of the vendors pinned me down as I was leaving the park.

"Can you help me out?" he asked. "I'm *this* close!" The smell of alcohol and unwashed privates rose up off him like bayou swamp gas.

"This close to what?"

He opened his hand and showed me the six or seven quarters in his palm. "A Big Mac," he said. "I just need—"

I slapped a dollar bill into his hand. "Here you go. Don't you buy any more juice with that."

The day was getting away from me. I ran over to Aubrey's hair guy, who bitched and fussed about the lack of notice but wound up giving me a terrific super short haircut.

Back at home, I mixed and matched every piece of clothing I owned. Finally I settled on—surprise—all black. A reliable old skinny dress that showed off my butt and legs but wasn't too dressy.

Shit, why should I sweat it? Dan would probably be turning more eyes than I would anyway.

We were having dinner, of course. But our first stop was a little hole-in-the-wall theater in Hell's Kitchen, where an old friend of Dan's was having his play done. "Don't worry," Dan had assured me. "It's only one act. And funny, not heavy."

He didn't lie. I laughed out loud a couple of times; I'd seen lots worse. Even with the obligatory author meet and greet, we were out of there and claiming our corner table at the French seafood restaurant on King Street less than ninety minutes after the curtain went up.

It smelled just right in there: garlic! butter! Coltrane on the sound system. Low lights anointed Dan's skin—and mine, if I was lucky—like an adoring handmaiden in a Renaissance painting.

I laid down one rule. "No talking about me when I was Daddy's favorite whiz kid."

"I can live with that," he said. "I'd much rather hear about your latest adventure in Paris anyway," he said.

Oh no, I told him firmly. That subject was also taboo. The last thing I wanted to do was relive my busted affair with Andre, let alone the Vivian nightmare.

His curiosity about my Paris trip made me realize that Daddy must have kept the story of Vivian's death a secret from him. So maybe he and Hinton weren't quite so tight as I had thought. Maybe Dan didn't even know "Eddie" had a sister.

We still found plenty to talk about over our funky bouillabaisse, endive salad, and house red. Like both of us often being lonesome and desperate as the only child. Both of us often being lonesome and desperate as black Ivy Leaguers—him some ten or twelve years before me. Both of us having a taskmaster for a father, a striver for whom failure was not an option—not for himself and not for his child.

I was letting my guard down. Maybe even showing off a little. It was risky to tell him about playing on the street. Neither of my parents knew about it. But I did it anyway. I knew he'd never rat me out to my father. He was too proud of his image as the good guy grown-up.

"Are you serious!" was his immediate reaction to my revelation. Equal parts shock and admiration.

Just the kind of response that little Nan craved.

I was off and running with stories about the fantastic assortment of characters I'd met on the street; the narrow escapes from muggers; the all-night parties with musicians and assorted other fiends; the sax player I'd picked up who ended up dead on my kitchen floor. Escapade after escapade, any one of which would curl my daddy's hair if he knew about it.

I painted myself as a cross between La Femme Nikita and Edith Piaf. Danny Boy was eating it up. Much raucous laughter emanating from our little corner.

"That's incredible stuff, Nan. You're really fierce."

I probably batted an eyelid or two.

"No, I mean it," he said. "You're so different from the picture I had of you. I mean, based on what I know about Eddie—and the things he says about you."

"You thought I'd be a black debutante, didn't you? A real BAP."

He fumbled for a politic answer.

"That's okay, I forgive you," I said. "I figured you for one, too."

Yes, I'd say my guard was definitely lowered. Somehow it no longer seemed important to dislike Dan Hinton just because my father did like him.

A mustachioed waiter went whizzing by with the dessert cart. Maybe a real femme on a first date would pass on dessert. But I got a good look at that pear tart and I knew I had to have it.

We shared it, laughing all the way through the last dollop of cream. I saw Dan raise his hand. But he wasn't calling for the check, or even for that end-of-the-night espresso. Instead he ordered another bottle of wine, with my hearty approval.

I was just as agreeable when he moved out of his chair and onto the small banquette with me.

We were only one glass into the new bottle when he mentioned that he was divorced.

"She left you, you said?"

He nodded.

"So—what was the matter with her?"

He took my fingers and kissed them lightly, and thanked me for saying that.

It took a long time for him to release my hand. He didn't let go, in fact, until after he had kissed me lightly on the mouth. So very lightly that in the kiss there was just as much *hello, dear cousin* as there was sexual interest. The thing sent a tiny tremor across my top lip. I didn't kiss back, I didn't not kiss back.

I had a bit more wine and then said, "You've been with a lot of women, haven't you? Had sex with a lot of women, I mean—to be blunt."

I could see him calculating, trying to figure what kind of answer I wanted to hear.

In the end he merely shrugged and said, "Yeah."

Well, that was honest. Kind of like my father—you gotta tell the truth even when it might work against you, and certainly without regard to how it might affect anybody else.

"Is that what happened with your marriage—too many other women?"

"We didn't break up over sex," he said, and I thought I caught a trace of patronization in his tone. "From the very beginning Michele and I had an understanding about attractions to other people. Michele was very enlightened about it."

Loosely translated: I was a fiend.

So Michele merely smiled and said skip that lipstick, eh? Ha.

I averted my head until I could wipe the smirk off my lips. Was I being unfair? People were hard on pretty men. It just seems so difficult to believe anything they say. Maybe it was an especially thorny problem for pretty black men, a lot of whom— let's face it—don't give too much of a shit whether you believe them or not. They know you're going to give it up anyhow, am I lying?

My attention had wandered. Dan was winding up his explanation of why he and the Mrs. split.

We got back to more immediate matters: a police raid on the wrong apartment that had ended in the death of a young man and his girlfriend, the names we gave as children to our imaginary siblings, did I really hate my dad's wife, Amy, or was it just the idea of her, what did I think of Wynton Marsalis.

It was late, one-thirty, when we paid up and left the restaurant. The manager bid us good night and bolted the door behind us.

We stood on the sidewalk, close together, not talking.

After a while he drew me to him, another kiss, not much cousin in that one.

"Should I put you in a cab?" he asked.

I thought about it for a second and then shook my head.

"Walk you home?"

"We could walk," I said, "but not home."

He didn't quite know what I meant. Even so, sexual anticipation flicked on in his eyes. I couldn't blame him. This was the moment when two people who've had a great evening together decide yes or no.

"I don't think you should see me home," I said.

"Why?"

"Because I'd probably ask you upstairs and jump straight into the sack with you."

"And that would be bad because . . . ?"

I laughed.

"Is it because of Eddie? Because I work for him?"

"Believe me, it's not that. I just—shouldn't—tonight," I said. "Look, we're only a few blocks from where my friend Aubrey works. I think I'll stop in over there. Maybe I'll spend the night at her place."

Gentleman Dan pushed no further. We turned south on Sixth Avenue. The wind nipped mildly at his open top coat and he kept me near to him with an arm over my shoulder.

"This is it," I said when we arrived at Caesar's Go Go Emporium.

"Are you serious!" he asked for the second time that evening.

"Yes," I said. "This is where Aubrey works. Exotic dancing, I think they call it."

Caesar's was as lurid as ever. Dirty windows outlined in blinking red bulbs, the vile back beat of disco music booming out through the door and onto the street.

"Gross, isn't it?" I said.

He had the weirdest grin on his face.

"I'm safe going in by myself," I told him. "They've got bouncers up the wahzoo in here. Besides, what if Aubrey's on now? You'll get one look at her bod and forget all about me."

"Not a chance," he said.

Shock. Puzzlement. Titillation. All there on his face.

Was I enjoying this. At last, *I* was the cool kid who was always leading everybody else into sin.

"Why don't you call it a night, Dan. I'll speak to you."

"I'm going in with you."

We made our way through the smoke-filled room. Men. Everywhere you turned. Young and old. Most of them drunk.

Dan said, straining to be heard above the din, "The mayor doesn't like strippers. What's your friend going to do if they start enforcing the law about places like this?"

I thought about it for a minute, and shrugged. "Maybe Alvin Ailey?"

As we were laughing about that, we heard a squeal of delight from somewhere behind us. "Smash! What up?" the voice said.

I turned to see Justin hurrying toward us.

Now, I would have predicted that a drink-and-chat meeting between Dan Hinton and the always outrageous Justin might well turn into a major surrealist event. But I was wrong. Mostly because Justin fell into near rapturous silence and let Dan do most of the chatting. By God, Dan Hinton had, like me, been raised by some rock-solid middle-class Negroes: he could keep up a polite line of small talk with just about anybody—even while they were staring at his crotch.

About a quarter to three, I convinced Dan to go home. I was exhausted and wanted to lie down in Aubrey's dressing room until she was changed and ready to leave. She was so busy that night she didn't even know I was in the house. But, I said teasingly to Dan, "I'll introduce you to her next time."

He kissed me good night like a rutting musk ox. I suppose the endless parade of naked female flesh, together with the testosterone in the air and the mild attack of homosexual panic that Justin had probably evoked, all contributed to his fervid embrace.

So ended my dream date.

Justin wore a filthy expression.

"Down, boy," I said. "The live sex act is over."

"Child, where did you get that man?" he said. "You must be

paying Mama Lou time and a half. I want that fucking doll back, you hear me?"

"Put your tongue back in your head, J." Aubrey was suddenly at my side. "Nanette, where did you get that man who just left out of here?"

LAST DANCE, like the song says.

The naked girls were all finished for the night and the cleaning people were sweeping the floor and stacking the chairs.

What time was it when I ate dinner? Nine or so. I had no business being hungry again, but there I was at the bar sharing an order of moo goo gai pan with Justin. The Chinese place off Canal Street never closed.

Aubrey was backstage cleaning herself up.

"Love is in the air," J said with a sigh, making his chopsticks do a little dance across the bar surface. "Mama Lou is working those roots."

"Oh, you think so, huh?"

"Yes, I do. Me and Kenny. You and Daniel. Love is all around and you're gonna make it after all, Smash-up. We're going to have a fabulous holiday season."

"Yeah. Fa-la-la."

"Speaking of Madam Lou and her magic, is there any news since our little enterprise uptown?" he asked. "Still trying to prove that Ida Williams was deliberately offed?"

"Still trying to find out exactly what happened. Ida wasn't exactly Miss Jane Pittman, turns out. She'd been in prison. Loveless doesn't think I'm quite so crazy now for being suspicious. I don't know much about the investigation. This pain-in-the-ass cop I know is supposed to be keeping me up to date on things. But I had to do something for him first. He's kind of got me over a barrel."

Raised eyebrow. "Sounds promising."

"Don't you ever stop, J?" I threw the fortune cookie at him.

"Okay. I'll stop. Are you ready for our next adventure?"

"What adventure is that?"

"Girl, don't pretend like you forgot about it."

"I'm not pretending. What are you talking about?"

"We're putting on the feedbag with Kenny tomorrow. You know—lunch? Crab cakes? Champagnes? You promised you'd go. He's taking us to Miss Mary's, our fave fag bar and grill."

"I did? Tomorrow? Oh, listen, J. I don't have a lot of time for drunches these days."

In an appeal for pity I added, "I'm really beat, man. I thought I'd sleep in tomorrow and then try to run down that old clipping we found, the one from that Cleveland newspaper."

"You *promised*, Smash-up. Kenny's going to be crushed if you don't."

"Okay, okay. Champagne it is."

"Not champagne—*champagnes*."

"All right, Tinkerbell. As long as the grapes don't come from New York States."

CHAPTER 10

I REMEMBER YOU

JUSTIN LIVED IN THE East Village, not far from me, maybe ten minutes walking. But I'd never been to his apartment and he had never been to mine.

Knowing his campy self, I expected not so much an apartment as a theme park. And the theme might have been anything from Motown to Bette Davis to gay serial killers. But, just like the way things turned out at Ida's apartment, I was totally off the mark.

His place was off Avenue A, on the fifth floor of a well-maintained old building with rococo ironwork across the lobby and the elevator doors. The apartment was sparsely furnished in restful colors playing off one another like a wry take on a Japanese tea ceremony: lapsong souchong, bitter brown, strong green tea, mint, celadon, eggshell. One or two lovingly restored antique pieces. In the front room, rice paper shades admitted that muted but strangely tactile light peculiar to the Lower East Side.

I'd told Justin I would pick him up about eleven-thirty and

we'd catch a cab over to the West Side where Kenny worked, at the southern end of Hell's Kitchen.

I oohed and aahed over his gorgeous all-nickel bathroom while he put the finishing touches on his outfit: he had to find a pair of socks that picked up that speck of color in his tie.

"By the way, what happened," I asked in the taxi, "to break your unbroken record with boyfriends? I thought you only dated black men or Italians."

"I know. Ain't it funny? I'm with a regular white-bread guy who could just as well be me. I met him at Mother Mary's one night and—bang zoom—I was in love. You know what I mean?"

I only nodded. Not because I wasn't listening. And not because I didn't care about his love-at-first-sight gushings. I had suddenly choked up. I was thinking about Andre. Thoughts about him and Paris and our time together there came at me that way, in quick hurtful bursts.

I pushed those memories away, hard, and looked over at Justin.

"Aside from all the jokes, you love him, do you?" I asked.

"Yeah, I guess I do. He's just a palooka who takes my money and makes me call him honey. But he's my palooka."

"He borrows money from you?"

"A few bucks. When he's between jobs. The boy is naturally extravagant. I like that in a man."

"Well, I hope you know what you're doing."

He leaned in close and said, "Baby, I don't care."

I did a loud, bad imitation of Lady Day—"*O mah man, I love him so, he'll nevuh know*"—and got a frightened look from the driver in the rearview.

MISS MARY'S WAS a welcome refuge from the grunge of the street. The unmistakable aroma of martinis hit us as we swung in the door.

Kenny slid out of the booth to greet us. He wore a finely cut jacket over a black T-shirt and dark pants. Light, close-cropped hair. That lanky Midwestern look. About the same age as Justin—well, J had never specifically revealed his age to me, but I figured him for thirty-nine or forty. Anyway, as J had told me, Kenny was a lot like him, even down to the hint of hard living in the corners of his eyes.

Justin began to introduce us, but Kenny hushed him. He put a friendly arm through mine and said, "You must be the Smash-up. J talks about you and Aubrey so much, I'd know you anywhere."

I was taken aback, balking instinctively at a stranger using that stupid nickname for me. I looked at Justin, who was beaming.

"Nice to meet you, Kenny," I said.

"So you're the great jazz musician," he said.

Great? I thought about it for a minute and then realized that Justin, not to speak of Kenny, had never heard me play a note. "I think you got me mixed up with some other Smash-up."

"Oh, don't be so modest. Justin says you're going to be famous someday. If you're famous, you're great, right? Just don't forget us little people when you get your record deal and you become a legend."

"A legend."

"For sure. Black beauty playing for pennies on the rough streets of New York. Can't you just see the poster? We'll shoot you on the Bowery; outside of one of those fancy bars where the models drink these days; you'll be wearing a leather jacket over your bra. I do a little PR work on the side, you know."

"What does PR stand for—Puerto Ricans?" Justin teased.

"Shut up," Kenny said.

"Did I mention," Justin said in a confiding tone, "that Kenny is the tiniest bit hyper?"

Suddenly it didn't seem all that presumptuous of Kenny to

call me Smash-up. What the hell, I thought, it's better than Cueball.

It never occurred to me that J talked to other people about me. He had this diva worship thing going with Aubrey. But I always thought he considered me little more than a mascot. I hadn't even noticed it, but over the last year or so Justin and I were getting to be real friends.

And so the "champagnes" began to flow. I had worried needlessly about the provenance of the grapes. We were sampling the wares of my favorite widow, old lady Cliquot, and getting soundly smashed.

An hour and a half later we had still not even glanced at the menu.

Kenny stopped abruptly midway through telling me about the trip to Cancun he was trying to talk Justin into. "I almost forgot!" he exploded. He then dropped his voice to a stage whisper. "I want to hear the latest on this thing you and J pulled in that old voodoo lady's apartment. Did you crack the case?"

"Hardly. But I did get a date out of it, indirectly."

"Date ain't the word, honey. That man is . . ."

I couldn't help grinning. "He is fine, isn't he? But as far as cracking any cases . . . I still don't know shit."

"You'll find something soon, Smash-up," Kenny assured me. "J says you're super cool and smart."

"Oh yeah? I guess that's why I'm carrying a copy of this guy Miller's picture around like some kind of jerk," I said. "I've been flashing it around like they do on TV."

I pulled out the photo of Miller and Ida.

Kenny took the print from me and looked at Miller's self-infatuated expression.

"Granted, he's a handsome devil," I admitted. "And he knows it. I've looked at that stupid photo so many times, I'm starting to feel like I know him from somewhere."

Kenny spent several minutes studying it, then commented, "He'd be older now, right? I mean, that lady, Ida, was much older than she is here, so he would be, too."

"Oh yeah. And I keep wondering if he's still good-looking. Black men don't always age well. 'Specially if they drink."

"Speaking of drinks," said Justin, "let's get another bottle."

"I'm sold," I said merrily. But at the same time I noticed that Kenny was holding the photo up to the light, turning it this way and that.

"What are you doing with that, Kenny?" Justin asked. "Don't tell me he's an old PR client of yours."

"Not exactly."

"What does that mean—'not exactly'?" I asked.

"He's just fucking with you, Smash-up," said Justin. "Kenny, I know you're high, but that's really not funny. That woman did get killed, after all."

"It might be funny in a different way," he answered. "I think I know this guy."

Justin and I spoke in chorus: "Say what?"

"I don't mean I *know* him. I mean I think I've seen him."

"You're serious," I said.

"Yes. And I can even top that—he's a sister."

"Shut up," Justin said, waving Kenny off.

I put my glass down and grabbed Kenny by his coat sleeve. "You're not fucking with me, are you?"

"No, I'm telling you. There's a guy comes in here a lot. A real closet case. Says he's not *personally* queer—he just hangs in here because he's got an office up the block and this place is so convenient. He comes here for the french fries. Right. Look around you, this place is Gay Central Station.

"He's always chatting some young thing up, passing his business cards around, telling people he's a producer—a music promoter. He's got a bigger line of bullshit than J and me put together."

"And you're telling me this gay producer is the man in this picture?"

"No, no, no. Listen a minute. The guy I'm talking about is white, and he can't be more than thirty-five. His name is Lyle. Lyle . . . Something. The thing is, he brought this man in the picture in here—I'm almost positive it was him—two or three times. A great-looking older black man. They sat right there at the end of the bar and they were talking mighty close. Real intense. I couldn't hear what they were saying. And believe me, I tried."

"Is this possible?" I asked no one in particular.

J shrugged, staring at Kenny as if still trying to determine whether he was putting us on.

He wasn't. The bartender with the gym body had one of those business cards. I grabbed Kenny roughly.

THE OFFICE WAS ONE cramped windowless room on a high floor of a commercial building on Forty-third between Ninth and Tenth Avenues.

Lyle Corwin was standing behind his desk talking on a cordless phone. He waved at us and gestured that he'd be done in a minute. White-bread hip. That was his look. Black Levi's, Fruit of the Loom V-neck, J.Crew blazer. And, unfortunately, a ponytail.

He was alone in the office. That made sense. I wouldn't imagine he'd have the money to pay a receptionist.

Lyle recognized Kenny right away. The two of them shook hands warmly. He was every bit as cordial to me when we were introduced.

"How're things in Miss Mary's today?" he asked.

"You know," said Kenny, "popping as ever."

Things remained friendly indeed until Kenny stated our business. It was he who presented the photo to Lyle and asked if he knew where we could find the gentleman pictured. Since he had been seen in Lyle's company, we thought he might be a client of his.

Lyle looked down at the photo and said, "I don't have a clue what you're talking about, man."

Silence fell in the dusty room.

I spoke up then. "Really?" I said. "Would you mind taking another look? This is an old shot of him."

He merely shook his head. "No. Like I said, no idea."

Kenny laughed nervously. "But I saw him up close, Lyle. He brushed past me when he left Mary's that last time."

"No, he didn't. Because there was never anybody like that in Mary's. At least not with me."

Kenny's hand went to his hip then. "Oh, I'm just a dizzy queen making this shit up, right?"

Lyle turned to me then. "I'm pretty busy here. Thanks a mil for dropping by."

I took Kenny's arm and led him toward the door without another word.

"Maybe you ought to get a new scrip, Kenny," Lyle said as we crossed the threshold.

Kenny tensed and turned back to him. "What did you say, Miss Thing?"

"A new scrip," Lyle repeated at high volume. "Not for your lady pills. For your eyeglasses."

"I do not wear glasses, you clueless fairy."

"Nice to meet you, Lyle," I called, and slammed the door shut behind us.

Justin was waiting for us back at the bar.

"No good, huh?" he said.

"No good," I echoed.

"Well, lover?" he asked Kenny. "Did we get a wrong number or what?"

He hesitated before answering. "I don't know. Maybe. I can't be a hundred percent sure. But the next time that punk shows his face in here I'm going to read him like a family Bible."

"You do that," I said. "Read him for me, too."

"What do you think, Smash-up?" Kenny asked. "I say he's lying. Even if I did make a mistake about that man, Lyle didn't act right."

"I'm with you there," I said. "But I don't know what we can do about it now."

"We can order crab cakes," Justin said. "We never got around to eating."

"I know. But I've got to go, fellas. Catch you later."

I don't know who gave me the stronger hug—Justin or Kenny. But, just as I left, the latter gave me a big smile and mouthed the word "Sorry."

It's a long walk from Hell's Kitchen to my place. But I needed the exercise. I walked fast.

If only my brain could have kept pace with my feet as I hustled along in those ugly old-lady shoes I love so. I was thinking, to be fair about it, but just not fast enough. And not far enough ahead.

WAS IT PMS?

Who can say why we fixate on a particular thing at a particular time?

All I wanted was a tuna sandwich. A huge smelly one, made with Italian tuna packed in high-quality olive oil, dripping with mayo, bursting with chopped onion and hard-boiled egg and chunks of tart green apple. And a ripe tomato sliced really paper thin; it could have tomato, but no lettuce. I wanted that on a hero, see, along with the giant-size bag of potato chips, the bag that's so big you're ashamed to meet the checkout girl's eyes, and, oh yeah, I was getting my period all right, a Coke. I never drink Cokes.

Of course the corner deli didn't have such a sandwich. Nor did any of the cool new minimalist cafés. So I was forced to shop for all those ingredients before coming back to the apartment, where there was next to nothing in the refrigerator.

What was there was one message from Leman Sweet and one from Dan Hinton.

Leman wanted to meet at Aubrey's place again that evening. Only he didn't say he "wanted" to and he didn't ask if I was free. He said, "I gotta" and "you gotta."

Dan's message walked the thin line between cuteness and genuine pornography. It looked like it was going to happen between us. Only a matter of when. Soon, I estimated. Not tonight, but soon.

I satisfied my shameful lust for that sandwich, put on some music—eight lamentations by Abbey Lincoln, including an excoriating "Love for Sale"—and worked my way down to the bottom of the chips. Then, tired as hell, I went to bed. It was only 3 p.m.

IT WAS A DEEP, worried sleep running riot with dread-filled dreams. The clock showed six when I pulled myself awake.

A quick shower. Fresh shirt. Grab Disley and Mama Lou. Out the door.

The doorman at Aubrey's knew me. He only tipped his hat as I rushed by him. I used my key to get inside the apartment. It was one of *the* surprises of my life to find Leman waiting for me on the sofa, stuffing his face with Famous Amos reduced-fat chocolate chips.

"You gonna stand there all night, girl? Come on in," he said, beckoning me.

"Well, thanks so much, Leman. Nice place you have here."

He snorted. "Aubrey had to leave. She said I could wait for you."

Holy mackerel. Was everybody insane? Or was I? Aubrey let Sweet remain alone in her apartment? I couldn't quite wrap my mind around it. Yet, here he was. Okay, Ernestine, I thought, enough said. Yes, I had used my friend unconscionably in asking her to be bait for the lovesick Leman Sweet; I wanted her to string him along, keep him from being so hard on me. But this was too much to ask.

"Well, what you looking at?" Leman asked resentfully. "Let's get to work."

"Work? Just a second, Sweet. I've got to tell you something first."

"What?"

"It's about you—about you and Aubrey. The thing is, if I were you, I'd forget about trying to get with her. You know?"

"I don't know what you talking about, Cueball. But skip it for now. I've got to talk to you about something."

"Ida? They know who killed her. Is that it?"

"Just sit down and shut up for a minute. Just listen."

I reached for the cookies.

"I told you what happened to that boy Black Hat, the kid caught in the crossfire of all that rap war shit. The theory of the case is, the money people at the big labels are feuding, eliminating each other. It's a solid theory. Like I said, he was small potatoes, so that lets him out as the intended target of a hit.

"But we have to run down every possibility—every angle—before closing the books. At least, that's what my squad is trying to do with the pitiful resources we have. Black Hat had parents with major bucks, so you can believe we're under some pressure to find out who killed him.

"But we're doing the same kind of thorough probing and prying number for all the victims. Not just following the main theory of the case but checking out any kind of off-the-wall angle we can think of. Interviewing family members. Checking out any big debts the vic might have had. Drug dealers. Jealous girl-friends. Jealous former boyfriends of girlfriends. Whatever.

"It just so happens that before he joined up with that crew of rappers Black Hat had a bad falling-out with his parents over money. Black Hat wanted them to bankroll his career as a song-writer and performer. His daddy has plenty of green, but not for that. He told Black Hat to forget it, in no uncertain terms. Jacob and Lenore Benson had given that boy a million-dollar education and he was an honor student at a fancy music school in Boston. But he wanted to hang with Phat Neck and Junior G and them and be a rap star. His daddy wasn't having it. Finally Black Hat dropped out of school, which made Jacob and Lenore Benson even madder.

"Black Hat turned his back on Jacob and Lenore and they turned away from him. Okay. A falling-out between a son and his folks. Nothing unusual in that story. But it usually doesn't end in murder. They were still feuding when he was killed. The Bensons never saw him again."

He stopped the story just long enough to go into the kitchen for something to drink.

"That is a sad story," I remarked when Leman returned with his glass of milk. "It doesn't really explain those things Felice said to his parents about getting revenge. But surely that's what she was talking about—their disrespect for his music, for what he wanted to do."

"I guess. But like I told you before, she was so upset nobody knew what she was talking about. At any rate, it don't matter no more what she meant. That's not what we're here for," Leman said.

"What are we here for, now that you mention it?"

"Just keep listening. We asked the families of the victims to provide us with all kinds of personal things connected to the victims—like datebooks, old address books, bank deposit slips, diaries, tax records—stuff like that. Any kinda thing they can think of. One thing we got from the Bensons was a videotape of the last family party Black Hat went to. Some of his school friends were there. So was Felice. I want you to take a look at it."

"What for? I don't know any of those people."

"Just take the tape and put it in the VCR."

I took the video he thrust at me and dutifully powered up the VCR and the TV set.

"Nice little apartment," I said, in a massive understatement. The place looked damn deluxe. The amateur cinematographer did a pan of the living room windows. A mighty fine view of the East River. A buffet table laden with fantastic-looking food. Magnificent baby grand with candelabra. Various groups of well-heeled folks posed in front of a baronial fireplace, waving congenially at the camera.

"Is that Black Hat?" I asked Leman.

"Yeah. That's him."

"Looks like a sweet boy. That must be Felice next to him."

He nodded. "And over there on the left are Jacob and Lenore."

"All very nice, Leman. But I don't get it."

"Hit the Pause button," he commanded.

I did.

"Look up there, near that white-haired dude's head. See there? On the mantelpiece?"

I got up from my seat and walked close to the set. I stared where he had directed my eye—and stared, and stared.

Oh yeah. That was the money shot all right.

At last I returned to my chair, too shaken to talk.

On the vast mantelpiece in the Benson apartment were exact replicas of Mama Lou and Dilsey, along with at least half a dozen of their cousins.

Ida Williams's dolls were decorating the majestic home of Jacob and Lenore Benson.

"What the hell does it mean?" I asked when I got my breath back.

"It means," he said, "that you and me ain't looking into two different crimes anymore, Cube—two different cases. It means we're on the same case. God help me."

"Yeah," I said, "God help us. What now?"

"I gotta find Felice Sanders. Now. And you gotta help me."

CHAPTER 11

IT SHOULDN'T HAPPEN TO A DREAM

AND SO IT APPEARED that voodoo, like the blues, would always be with us.

Try as I might, I couldn't seem to get away from Mama Lou and Dilsey and this whole world of mad synchronicity.

Everywhere I turned, Event A segued into Event B. Individual X, as unlikely as it seemed, was somehow connected to Individual Y.

And the further away I was pulled from the Ida Williams case, the closer I was to it. It was all a strange circle.

"I want to meet the Bensons," I had told Leman as we sat in Aubrey's living room with the telltale video still in the machine. "I mean, I don't *want* to, but I think I need to. Can I?"

"Why? You think they know where Felice Sanders is?"

"No, it's not that," I said, fidgeting. I opened the glass cigarette box on the coffee table and helped myself to one of Aubrey's vile menthols.

"Then what do you want to see them for? I told you, girl. The Sanders kid is now top priority for us. Even more than the Black Hat thing. We have to find her."

He and I exchanged a quick, nervous look. "You think something bad's happening to her, don't you, Leman?"

"Damn straight I do."

"Yeah, so do I."

Sweet probably couldn't articulate just how he knew that Felice was in danger. But then, he didn't need to. It simply made sense that she would be. The appearance—the synchronicity—of those dolls spoke volumes. Poor little Black Hat is murdered, supposedly caught in the crossfire of a drive-by shooting—a hit. Poor old Ida Williams is murdered, supposedly caught in the crossfire of a shooting in a posh Manhattan eatery. The dolls, which looked for all the world like Ida's handiwork, turn up at the home of Black Hat's parents. And now Black Hat's would-be widow, Felice Sanders, is missing.

Voodoo or not, it was too much synchronicity to be ignored.

"I want to check out those dolls on the mantelpiece, make sure they're still there, for one, and maybe try to identify them positively as Ida's work. Besides that, the Bensons may not know where Felice is, but maybe they've heard from her more recently than her mother or Dan Hinton. I mean, she did make some weird threats against them, didn't she? Maybe she's trying to carry them out."

He thought about it for a few seconds. "Okay. It may not be such a bad idea. I'll tell them to expect you and I'll give you their phone and address. Yeah—you probably do know how to talk to people like the Bensons."

"Sure I do. We'll have a tea party."

Damn him. I had thought for a few minutes that Sweet was admitting he and I were on the same side. He had said "we" had to find Felice. It seemed, just for a few minutes, that he was acknowledging some kind of kinship between us—maybe even flattering me with the implication that I could be of real help in this investigation—that I could put two and two together, like him.

"Okay, Cue, don't get up on that high horse a-yours. You can see the Bensons. Check out the 'authenticity' of those goddamn dolls. Which you know damn well are Ida's. But don't think I don't know what you're really up to. You still got your mind on the Williams murder. Trying to prove you were right about it. You still think you gonna be the one to break a case the police can't solve."

I began to protest, but he cut me off: "Just get in and out of there with any information that could help us out with the Felice thing. We don't have no more time to waste."

"All right, all right, all right."

But there it was again—what's going to help "us" out; "we" don't have time to waste. Man, did this guy run hot and cold.

"What are you going to do next, Sweet?"

"Talk to Missing Persons again. Then get over to Felice's mother's place. I got things to check out, too."

"I bet," I said snottily. "Like whether Felice collected voodoo dolls. We were pretty stupid not to think of it before."

He looked at me and I could almost see something like a smile. "You ain't too dumb, girl. I'll give you that."

"You go ahead. I'll lock up here."

I CALLED THE BENSON HOME first thing the next morning. The housekeeper told me that Dr. Benson had already left for the hospital and the lady of the house was out for the day.

I reached Jacob Benson at the hospital where he was chief pediatric surgeon. It was not until I heard his cultured, even-toned voice that I realized how delicately I would have to broach the reason for my call. He was, after all, a parent still in mourning for his child.

"Good morning, Dr. Benson. My name is Nanette Hayes."

"Yes, Ms. Hayes. Detective Sweet left a message telling me to expect your call. What can I do for you?"

I decided it was best to get right to the point. "It's about your son's fiancée, Dr. Benson. Felice Sanders. She hasn't been seen for some time now. I'm helping Sergeant Sweet in his inquiries."

I heard his deep intake of breath. "I don't understand," he said at last. "What happened to Felice?"

"She has officially been reported as a missing person, Dr. Benson. I wondered if you might have seen her since—uh—lately."

"No." His voice dropped then. "I—Well, I hardly know what to say."

"Dr. Benson, I'm sorry to be reminding you of these painful things, but it would help a lot if you could see me for a few minutes today."

Again he hesitated before speaking. "I'm not sure I'll be able to make any time to see you today. I'm scheduled to—"

"Yes, sir. I know how busy you must be. Actually, it would be best if I could drop in at your home this evening. Would that be convenient?"

"Oh. I suppose that's all right. But I don't know how it will help. We didn't maintain a friendship with Felice once Kevin was gone."

"I understand. Believe me, this shouldn't take more than fifteen minutes of your time."

"Very well. Do you have the address?"

"East Seventy-second, between York and the river. Twenty-first floor."

"Yes. All right. Some time after seven would be best."

"Thank you. I'll be there."

I don't know why the brief conversation left me feeling

scummy. But it did. Dr. Benson and his wife had gone through a horrific tragedy and understandably just wanted their privacy. I was going to their home to snoop and was feeling guilty about it. That was the long and short of it.

The faltering old radiators in my apartment were doing right by me as of late. But it was pushing my luck to sit around in my night things and no wrapper. I changed into pants and an old sweatshirt and hunted down some thick socks; put on Monk's *Straight, No Chaser* and then made espresso and scalded some milk.

I sat with my coffee listening to Charlie Rouse's impeccable work on "Japanese Folk Song." I'll get up and change the CD, I told myself, before that hymn plays—"Blessed Assurance" (although the CD lists the title as "This Is My Story, This Is My Song").

Did I have some kind of problem with hymns? No. Oh no. Andre and I used to listen compulsively to that beautiful tune in the little apartment we had on the rue Christine. Sometimes we would hold hands and sing the words as though we were in church together. There was a bunch of music that we'd listened to over and over—or played together—that I just had no heart for anymore.

But I didn't do it. I didn't change the CD. I forced myself to sit there and take it. If I was going to follow through with the Ida Williams case and help Leman Sweet find that missing girl, I had to stop being so fucking cowardly. Doing those things was going to require a lot more balls than listening to "This Is My Story"—or "I'll Be Seeing You" or "We'll Be Together Again" or any number of other tunes Andre and I had listened to, danced to, made love to.

I let the album play out and then put on more Monk—this time strictly solo. I turned the volume down a bit, though, because I had to make a couple of other phone calls.

First I was going to leave a message for Leman that it was on for tonight with me and the Bensons.

Then I was going to call Dan Hinton. I wanted to catch him before he left for work, while (I hoped) there was still a hint of sleep in his magnificent voice.

Yes. All right. Copping to it. Through with love but not through with sex.

"MUST GET AWFULLY COLD here with the wind coming off the river," I remarked to the doorman.

"That it does," he said. "But I don't mind that much. Kind of like the cold."

I guess his shift was just beginning, or perhaps he was just returning from his dinner break. He had just changed from street clothes into his uniform jacket, apparently. I caught sight of the very top of his white undershirt as he finished buttoning up.

I've got about a million New York doorman stories. They can be unspeakably snotty bastards. I could compile a list as long as your arm of the mean white guys who treated me like dirt when I showed up at the fancy buildings where they stood guard. Young ones, old ones, Irish ones, Italian ones, Latino ones, Jewish ones. Racist doormen are a kind of equal opportunity plague.

A lot of black doormen do not like colored folks making social calls in their buildings, either. Something about the fact of another Negro on the premises who isn't there as a babysitter or a repairman just makes them boil. I have a particularly vivid memory of one lawn jockey in red livery, the gatekeeper in a luxe building on Fifth Avenue and Ninth Street, where I was going to a party. It had taken every bit of my breeding not to use my sax to pop him in his shiny fucking teeth.

Anyway, unfriendliness was definitely not a problem with this door guy—MIKE, his name tag read. He was about the same age as Dan Hinton and he had the kind of blue eyes that were dreamy rather than scarifying.

"You look like you'd be nice and warm," Mike said.

"Excuse me?"

"You look nice and warm in that coat you're wearing. That's what I meant."

Another good-looking man coming on to me.

Ho hum.

"The Bensons are expecting me," I said serenely.

He checked the long sheet of paper on the desk. "Miss Hayes, right?"

"Yes."

"It is *Miss* Hayes, not Mrs.? Or am I out of luck tonight?"

I didn't answer. You cheeky bastard, I thought. Bet you don't earn your tips walking poodles. The housekeeper, or the maid, whoever it was I'd spoken to in the morning, had apparently gone home. It was Dr. Jacob Benson himself who admitted me.

Once we were out of the shadows of the doorway, I could take him in fully. He was right out of a 1920s daguerreotype—caffe latte complexion, James Joyce spectacles, wavy white hair and pencil mustache, ramrod posture in his pinstripe English-cut suit. I made a quick calculation in my head: Black Hat was only a kid nineteen or twenty years old—so his folks ought to be younger than mine. But the tall, beautiful man before me looked close to seventy.

Did I say my father was a stick? Dr. Benson made him look like RuPaul.

On one wall of the long corridor was a Benny Andrews painting that I remembered admiring in a catalogue. There were nine-foot-high bookcases with medical texts and journals lined up neatly. I saw a phone and answering machine setup on a gorgeous cherrywood secretary. And, out of the corner of my eye, I caught a flash of yellow-and-red fabric in a wooden display case. I willed myself not to stop and stare.

A second later, though, I got the chance to check it out up close. The hall phone rang as we were passing through, and Dr. Benson stopped and switched on the desk lamp. While he was giving instructions, apparently to someone from the hospital, I was able to confirm that the bright fabric was part of the costume worn by a ferocious-looking doll. Standing about two feet tall, she was the Mama Lou to end all Mama Lous.

Benson finished his call and joined me, but then he turned back into the hallway. "Forgive me. This will only take a moment," he said, and went back to the phone. A few seconds later I heard him ask for Nurse Peters and then hand down additional instructions.

He was helping me off with my coat when the phone rang yet again. I'd assumed that at his age he would be functioning mostly in an advisory capacity at the hospital, but he seemed to be as much in demand as any young medical hotshot.

"I'm very sorry about all these interruptions," the doctor said in his courtly manner.

"No, please. Go right ahead."

This time he didn't bother to pick up the receiver. He merely punched one of the many little buttons on the machine. He turned down the volume on the message being left. "There," he said wearily. "Now we should be all right. At least for a while."

I was shown into the huge living room with the panoramic view of the East River Drive and the water. He let me take it in for a minute and then asked, "May I give you a cocktail?" But then he retracted the offer immediately. "No, of course you won't drink. You must still be on duty."

"Duty?"

"I forgot for a moment that you're with the same Homicide detail as Detective Sweet."

I blinked moronically. Surely Leman had not represented—or misrepresented—me as a policewoman. Benson must not have listened to that message very carefully. But his mistaken assumption was an understandable one.

What to do now? Nothing, I decided.

"That's quite all right, Dr. Benson," I said mildly.

"You're very young," he noted. "You must have distinguished yourself in the department very quickly."

A modest shrug was my answer.

I pulled out my fifty-nine-cent notepad then. Not as good a prop as a badge, but I was improvising. "As I told you earlier, sir, Felice Sanders is missing. I understood you to say you spoke to her at least once after your son's funeral. Can you tell me when and where that conversation took place?"

It took him a few moments to answer me, and when he did his voice was lifeless. "Felice phoned me a week or two after the funeral. She said she wanted to apologize for—for some things she said at the service. Things said in anger."

"She had made some sort of threat, didn't she?"

"Yes. She was going on about our being to blame for what happened, berating Mrs. Benson and myself for not having had any faith in Kevin. For disrespecting him."

"That must have made you pretty upset."

He cleared his throat, looked at me mournfully.

"Didn't she say something about getting back at you?"

"Yes. She said she was going to show us up as fools who didn't understand him or his music. There were already plans to release his records—or whatever they call them these days."

Perhaps I was imagining it, but I thought I saw his eyes travel rather desperately around the room after he pronounced the word *music*, his searching glance coming to rest on one of two magnificent black Bose speakers. A man I once lived with, Walter Moore, was forever talking about the day when he would be able to afford them.

The story was that Black Hat had asked his father for money to bankroll his career as a rap musician. Jacob Benson had roundly refused him. I had no trouble seeing that. One look at the man told me he was no fan of hip-hop culture. He probably loathed the very idea of rap, found it degrading filth. I could hear them—father and son—arguing about it now. I could just hear the venerable Dr. Benson mocking his son for his aspirations and for the thuggish clothes he wore, railing against him for wasting his education and the opportunities his parents had worked so hard to afford him. As for the ridiculous name he had taken on—Black Hat—what the hell was wrong with his own name—Kevin Benson?

Yes, he'd probably said things like that, and more.

And God, what he wouldn't give now to relent and give Black Hat every cent he had in the world for whatever kind of music he liked. Let the boy call himself the Naked Ape, if that's what he wanted. Anything to have his child back.

"Did that threat have any meaning for you, Dr. Benson?"

"No. The girl was distraught. Of course we were upset at the scene she made, but she was—ah—grieving." He swallowed hard before going on. "Grieving, as we were. She asked for our forgiveness. And I gave it."

"Did Felice happen to say where she was calling from at the time?"

"I'm not sure I understand."

"Did she say she was staying with a friend? Calling from out of town? Anything like that?"

"No. I assumed she was at home with her mother."

"Do you know any of her friends? Someone she might be staying with?"

"No."

"And there has been no contact since the phone call?"

"None. As I told you earlier, we weren't close with her." He shook his head. "Don't misunderstand, Detective. It isn't that we have anything against the girl. It's just that she wasn't the girl we envisioned Kevin marrying. And who is to say that the marriage really would ever have— Well, what does all that matter now? I'm very sorry about her disappearance. Kevin . . . Kevin had feelings for her. I'm sorry out of respect for his memory."

That smarmy feeling was coming back. Dr. Benson was sagging, on the verge of weeping. I was ripping open a wound. Maybe more than one wound—I could just as easily write in my head the dialogue for the arguments he must have had with Black Hat over young Felice. I had to think of something to turn Benson in a different direction.

"I wonder," I said suddenly, "if I could have a glass of water."

"Yes, surely."

He rose from his seat quickly enough, but used his hand to brace his back as he walked toward the kitchen.

As soon as he rounded the corner, I hurried over to the fireplace. In addition to the ones in the display case, there must have been twelve dolls artfully arranged at the corner of the mantelpiece, the Dilsey and Mama Lou duplicates among them. Ida didn't sign her work, but I didn't see how these could have been made by anyone else. All the models I had seen on her folding table in Union Square were represented here.

There was also a sweet photo of Black Hat, arms around his mother, in a silver frame.

I was back in my chair when Dr. Benson returned. He handed me the water tumbler and I dutifully drained it.

"I was just admiring those figures above the fireplace," I told him. "They're charming. Where do they come from?"

He glanced over at the dolls. "I'm not sure. My wife buys

them from a seamstress she knows, I believe. They became fast friends." He nearly laughed then. "She has a mania for them, as you can see. They're everywhere you look in the apartment."

"They're so interesting. Do you think she'd mind if I asked her for the lady's name?"

"Lenore is out tonight."

"Do you expect her back soon?"

"Not for some time."

"I see. Well, actually I think that takes care of the questions I had for you, Dr. Benson. I'd just like to add my condolences."

"Thank you, Detective Hayes. I wish you would—"

He stopped there.

"What is it?" I asked.

"The girl's mother—she must be suffering over what's happened. I know she must be. I'd like to . . . Would you . . . if you speak to her—"

"Yes, I will, Dr. Benson. I'll tell her you're sorry about Felice."

I waited a few minutes out in the hall before calling the elevator. Don't have kids is what I was thinking.

Downstairs, Mike folded the magazine he was reading so I couldn't see the cover. I was betting it was some sex maniac crap.

I didn't give him time to take up where he left off with me. I said good night on the fly and was through the revolving door before he could speak. But then I stepped back inside the lobby, and caught him reaching for the magazine.

"You've come to your senses," he said. "I knew you'd be back."

I borrowed a phrase from Leman. "You're not too dumb, are you?"

He flashed a killer smile.

"And yes, it is *Ms*. Now, let me ask you a couple of questions, Mike."

"Okay."

"Did you ever meet Kevin's girlfriend?"

"No, I don't think so."

"I see. One other thing: the Bensons must have been real shaken up when they lost their son."

He nodded grimly. "I feel sorry for them. They're decent people."

"What does Lenore Benson do with her days—surf Fifty-seventh Street?"

"I don't follow you."

"You know, shopping. I mean, she doesn't seem to spend much time at home. Am I right?"

"Not lately she doesn't. But she's not out shopping. That's for sure."

"You mean you know where she is?"

"Yes. I got a cab for them—that day."

"What day?"

He took a quick survey of the lobby before answering, "The day she lost it."

"Lost it? What did she lose?"

" 'It.' You know. He carried her out one day. She was stiff as a board and talking . . . crazy."

"You mean crazy for real."

He nodded. "Like I said, I whistled up a taxi. I heard him tell the cabbie they were going to Payne Whitney. She hasn't been back since."

Payne Whitney. That wasn't a chic new women's boutique. Nor was it an investment house. It was a famous, very expensive psychiatric facility with a view of the East River just as impressive as the one from the Bensons' living room.

CHAPTER 12

DEEP IN A DREAM

SHE CROSSED HER LEGS exactly the way a woman should.

Lenore Benson looked fabulous.

She also looked at least twenty years younger than her husband.

The exquisite dove-gray frock and luminous pearl necklace didn't hurt, but I had the feeling she would look fabulous in a flour sack. She was an immensely beautiful woman.

One glance told me why Jacob Benson chose her to be the woman on his arm at the Wealthy Negroes Ball. And the hostess for those important dinner parties with his medical colleagues. And the mother of his child.

My guess was that Lenore was a transplant from the South—one of those unreal black belles whose remarkable grace was an ironic legacy from the example-setting white belles who had trained and owned their ancestors, and sometimes blithely sent them to their deaths.

Very likely the salespeople at Bergdorf's greeted Mrs. B by name. Very likely she could identify a cold-meat fork at thirty paces. But she also headed literacy campaigns, ran a birth control clinic, and knew how long ham hocks should cook.

"Oh yeah. She's out of it all right."

Leman Sweet's words sounded crass, insensitive, true.

Whatever Mrs. Benson had been, wherever she was from, she was somewhere else now. Her statue-like placidity and the checked-out expression in her eyes told me so.

Sweet and I were watching her through the doors of the day-room. We were waiting for her psychiatrist to join us.

"Why do you think Benson lied?" I asked. "Well, not exactly lied. He just implied she was only out for the evening."

"Probably 'cause he thought it was none of your business," Leman said. "This headshrinker feels the same way. He won't say much and the law says he don't have to. But he can't stop the police from investigating a crime. We got a right to talk to anybody, no matter what shape they're in, if they might know something about a missing kid."

"Or a murder," I added.

"Yeah. Or a murder. Anyway, this doc says we can ask her a couple of questions, for all the good it's going to do. She's on a lot of cool-out medicine and sometimes she won't even talk to him."

A small white man with silver hair walked swiftly through a set of doors at the other end of the hall, heading toward us. The headshrinker, as Sweet called him, greeted us civilly enough, introduced himself as Doctor Paul Bergash. He would remain in the room, he informed us, while we questioned his patient. But we had to realize how profoundly unresponsive Mrs. Benson had been lately. Her son's death had sent her spiraling into the kind of depression she might never emerge from.

He held the door for me. Only when he placed his hand on my back and began guiding me into the sunny, tranquil blue room did I realize how hesitant I was to step inside. I had to admit, the "quiet room" gave me the willies.

But when Mrs. Benson looked up at us in that kindly grande dame way, I felt much better, almost at ease, almost normal.

Sweet said it was probably best that I do most of the questioning, I would know how to talk to "these people."

"Mrs. Benson, how do you do. I'm Nanette Hayes. This is Sergeant Sweet from the city police. Do you feel up to answering a few questions?"

"More oranges?" she said. "You're too kind."

For the next five minutes or so she had no response at all, not even an enigmatic one like the non sequitur we had just heard. But then something I said seemed to strike a chord.

"We're worried about something, Mrs. Benson. It's Felice Sanders. No one has heard from her for a long time. We thought maybe you might know where she can be reached. Do you remember when you last spoke with her?"

"Yes. Lovely prostitute. Oh dear, what did I say? I meant 'posture.'"

"What did she say when you spoke to her?"

"It couldn't be helped."

"What couldn't be helped?"

"Unsuitable, completely unsuitable."

I looked up at Bergash, whose face was unreadable.

"Please," I said, "we realize you're here to help Mrs. Benson, not us. But you do know this kid is missing, right? And it doesn't look so good for her. You realize that, right?"

"Yes."

"I'm asking you—did she really talk to Felice Sanders? Do you think Mrs. Benson knows what happened to the girl?"

His impassive face softened for a minute, but finally he just shook his head. "I can't help you."

When Sweet refused to stop staring at the doctor, he repeated his disclaimer: "I'm sorry. I don't know."

"I saw the beautiful collection of dolls you have at home," I said to Lenore Benson. "Could you tell me where to buy one?"

"Yes. She's a lovely woman. Very talented. Someone to talk to."

"Who is that?" I asked. "Do you mean Ida Williams?"

"All of them. There're so many to choose from."

"So many dolls, you mean?"

"Yes, they're lovely."

She reached out convulsively then, as if trying to catch one of those lovely oranges she had mentioned a while ago. It was then that I noticed the hatched marks across her wrists and up her arms. Leman saw them, too. Just as quickly as she had made the gesture, her hand was back in her lap and she was once again the picture of unearthly composure.

Leman spoke then: "Mrs. Benson, I have a photograph I'd like you to look at. Do you know who this man is?"

He placed the copy of Miller's photo into her hands.

"Julian! Good heavens, it's Julian. And doesn't he look well."

"You're identifying this man?" Leman asked.

"I should think I'd recognize Julian Bond when I see him, young man. He's sat at my table often enough." She handed the sheet back to Leman with a smile.

"Mrs. Benson, do you know a man by the name of Miller?" I asked.

When I got no answer, I added, "Or Lyle Corwin?"

"I'm sure his name is Julian, dear," she said, her flinty tone providing a hint of the steel magnolia she must have once been.

"I think we ought to wrap this up now, don't you?" I asked Sweet.

He nodded agreement, but then said, "Just a minute. Mrs. Benson, have you ever met a man named Dan Hinton? A friend of Felice's?"

I looked piercingly at him but said nothing.

I offered my hand to Lenore Benson and thanked her for speaking with us. She delivered her greatest line in reply to that.

She said, "In the end, we all do . . . don't we?"

It had not gone especially well, to use the kind of delicate euphemism Lenore herself might employ.

I was the one who had talked Sweet into this visit to Payne Whitney. He had said all along that it wouldn't pay—the shrink had told him on the phone the kind of shape Mrs. Benson was in. The sergeant was in a pretty foul mood now.

"*Dan Hinton?*" I said when we were out on the street again. "What do you mean pulling his name out of your ass like that? What have you got against him, huh?"

"Look, Cueball, we don't rule out anybody. I could have asked her about your fancy daddy, too, you know."

I wasn't going to rise to his class-baiting this time. "You could have asked her about Julius Caesar for all I care. What difference would it make? She probably knows him, too."

CHAPTER 13

IT'S ALWAYS YOU

I PICKED UP the ringing telephone just before the machine kicked in.

"Big Legs? Is that you?"

"Roamer?"

Of course it was Roamer McQueen, my very temporary colleague from the Omega gig. Even if I couldn't place their voices immediately, I could always keep my male acquaintances straight by their pet names for me.

"How're you keeping these days, Big Legs?"

"So-so, Roamer. You know."

"You know how to cook, girl?"

The question threw me for a minute. Where was this heading? "No complaints that I recall," I said at last.

"You know how to fix red beans and rice?"

"Forget it."

"Yeah, I thought as much. Why don't you come out and have something to eat with me."

"Thanks, but not today."

"Oh, come on, Nan. It'll make you feel better. I want to take you somewhere and show you off. Down at this place where my nephew cooks."

I paused before declining a second time. I thought I heard something in his voice, something that made me suspect this invitation wasn't just about home cooking.

"You want to tell me something, am I right?" I said.

"Yeah. We'll talk about it. Keep me company while I get something to eat."

"All right. Not for too long, though. I gotta get back home."

"Okay. And bring your horn."

"Where?" I asked.

Great Jones Street. Off Broadway. That was the *where*. The *what* was Texaco, a Southern-style restaurant I had never heard of before.

A black man in an expensive-looking gray raincoat stepped up quickly from behind and held the restaurant door open, cruising me like mad as we both walked in. He was my dad's age or older, but his glance was distinctly unfatherly. Why should I be surprised, though, given my current status as male magnet?

I returned the appraising look. He might have been up there in years, but the man had great skin and mesmerizing eyes. And he used them to hold mine for a while. I did not look away.

No, I don't have a jones for senior citizens. It's just that, for me, flirtation doesn't have to lead anywhere; it's all about the moment. I mean, I *am* French—sort of. Experience counts for a lot in a man, *n'est-ce pas*? That and self-confidence, which he seemed to have plenty of. It showed in his smile.

The thing that ended our moment was that belted raincoat. Once I got a good look at that, I was through. I don't care how much the thing cost, it always bums me when a man ties the belt on his raincoat that way—tight. I never met a guy who did that who was worth a damn.

"Eating by yourself today?" he asked.

"Not on your life, James Bond."

Texaco was one of those places desperate to replicate the ambience of a Louisiana lean-to way off Bourbon Street. Big Mama Thornton, Fats Domino, Johnny Ace on the jukebox. Old ads for Dixie Beer and beef jerky. Elvis memorabilia.

Only a few people were eating at tables, but the bar was full. Whole lot of smoking Marlboros and knocking back shots of Wild Turkey was going on. Baskets of hush puppies substituted for the usual free pretzels deal.

I figured Roamer's nephew would be straight out of central casting, too: big around the belly, white apron stained with hot sauce, and regulation gold tooth.

Lost that bet, except for the apron. I was introduced to Carl, who was willowy and rather ethereal looking, with perfectly normal incisors. His belly, incidentally, looked just fine to me. He set me up with some scrambled eggs while Roamer dug into his down-home vittles.

"You getting back on your feet, after that lady was shot like that?" Roamer asked.

"I'm trying. Looks like the story was deeper than even I figured. A cop I know was supposed to help me find out what really happened. But I got pulled into all kinds of crazy stuff. At this point I don't know who's helping who to find out what. It's all kinds of fucked up."

"What are you doing running around trying to play with the cops anyway? That's no job for you."

I sighed. "Yeah, I know."

"That's one of the things I wanted to talk to you about—jobs. I guess I'm going to have to be the bearer of bad news."

"Oh no." I put the square of cornbread I was about to butter back into the basket. "What is it?"

"The Omega gig is over. We're history."

"Damn. I knew it. Something told me you were going to say that."

"Yeah. They're closing. Brubeck says between the protection money and the taxes and the loans and now this killing, he's had it."

All I could do was snort. "Mama Lou strikes again. Any idea how you murder a doll, Roamer?"

"Murder a who?"

"Skip it. What are you going to do? You and Hank."

"That's the other thing I want to tell you. Hank and me are going out west for a couple of months. Cat we used to know is doing good with a little club in L.A. He asked us to come out there. It could turn into something permanent. I don't know."

"Oh, that's great, Roamer. You must be so happy."

"Sounds good, doesn't it?"

"Hell yeah."

"So have you got your passport in order?"

"Me?"

"Yeah, you. Why don't you come on with us?"

I was so moved I could barely answer him. "I'm incredibly flattered. But what about Gene?"

Surely Hank and Roamer were not going to drop their long-time friend Gene Price in favor of me.

"He'll come out when he gets well. The doctor and his old lady have laid down the law to him. He ain't going anywhere just now. See, we figured you'd go on taking Gene's spot. It couldn't hurt you to get a rep out on the west coast. You're unusual enough, being a girl sax and all, maybe it'll bring in the crowds even more. By the time Gene gets out there, you could be doing something else, have your own thing going. Shit, you could be one of them movie stars this time next year. Lots of things could happen for you. Who knows?"

Career decisions. Opportunity knocking. Smart move. Make it happen.

All phrases that were barely part of my vocabulary. Almost as if they weren't ordinary English words.

"God, Roamer, I don't know what to say."

"Say you're going home to pack your lacy pants and kiss the boys good-bye, Big Legs."

"But am I good enough to cut it—you guys think I am?"

"You know that old joke, don't you? Practice, honey, practice."

"When do you have to know?"

"About a week, I guess. You better think about it, Nan. But not too long."

I nodded. It was, not counting the Hollywood star thing, a lot to think about. Something else to think about. That's what I needed.

"You look funny," Roamer said. "If you don't eat that biscuit, I will."

"Help yourself," I said. "You know what I was just thinking? Do you know anything about the chitlin circuit? You know, the old black vaudeville acts. I don't mean from way back in the blackface-and-fright-wig days. I mean like closer to the tail end of that stuff—the fifties and sixties."

"Moms Mabley and Redd Foxx, and Nipsey Russell," he said between bites. "Before they let us into Vegas and all."

I knew those names dimly. I also knew who would have been able to give me chapter and verse on all of them: my old love, Andre, who had dedicated his life to chronicling black entertainers. But he wasn't here. And I probably wouldn't have need of this conversation if he was. Everything would be different.

"I guess I mean people like that," I said. "Anyway, you never heard of a team called Miller and Priest, did you?"

"Nah. Doesn't ring a bell. Who are they?"

"Too long a story."

Carl came over to the table then. "Can I hook you up with some more eggs, Nan?"

"No, thanks. They're real good, though. I'm just not hungry. Got a big dinner coming up tonight."

"Shit," Roamer snapped. "You're busy tonight, huh?"

I didn't understand why that should annoy him so.

"I thought you and Carl might go out," he explained.

"Thanks for looking out for me," Carl said, about three times as embarrassed as I was. He busied himself wiping at the table surface.

"By the way, Roamer, what did you have me bring the horn for? If I dare ask that question."

"For Carl. I wanted him to hear you. I told you I was gonna show you off. Besides, I don't like the jukebox in here. They always start off with Etta James, but before you know it, it's all Rolling Stones."

"I guess you think you're pretty irresistible, Roamer."

I started with "Trust in Me," not only one of Etta's great hits but, according to Roamer, his favorite song.

CHAPTER 14

DARN THAT DREAM

THE FOOD WAS GOOD on our second date, too. Only this time we dined in Brooklyn Heights. And Dan Hinton did the cooking.

The small talk—weren't we having luscious cool weather and how attractive his apartment was and didn't I look ravishing tonight—didn't take long. We were soon logging quality time kissing our way through cocktails.

The chicken was superb, not some bachelor fry-up with prepackaged seasonings. The vegetables tasted just harvested. French bread crisp as a new fifty from the bank. Okay, the napoleons were store-bought, but that didn't stop them from being wonderful, too.

Dan had opened the second bottle of wine and it was waiting for us out on the glass-enclosed deck.

Gorgeous man, gorgeous view, great food and wine, and, if I was any judge, the promise of some memorable sex. Ms. Hayes, semiprofessional hedonist that she is, was a happy girl.

At least that is what she was telling herself. But it wasn't true. It just wasn't true.

For a while there I was blaming Andre.

I found Dan desirable, to say the least. And man did he know where all the light switches were on a woman's body. But he wasn't Andre.

It took a while to realize even that wasn't the problem—not all of it, anyway.

But in the meantime, the two of us in one deck chair, Dan and I were delighting in all the preliminaries you could think up.

"I can hardly wait for you, Nan," he said, the lust in his grin outshining the candles on the table nearby. "You are such a nice big girl."

Not the least bit insulted, I laughed and asked him why that made him so happy.

It was marvelous to have a man looking right into my eyes that way, to have a man's hands on me in that way—I mean with tremendous heat and urgency but also with tenderness and a kind of friendship. The love you make with a one-time guy is just not like that.

Dan excused himself a few minutes later: To make sure the sheets were clean? Look for the Barry White LP? I took the opportunity to smooth out my skirt and indulge in another dab of stinky cheese.

He took a minute too long.

For it was while I was waiting for him to return, sipping my wine and looking up at the stars, that I hit on what was truly bothering me.

Damn that Leman Sweet. Damn him twice.

Dan joined me again, slipped his arm expertly around my waist. "Sky looks incredible tonight, doesn't it?" he said.

"Yeah, it does."

A few angel-light kisses on my ears and neck.

"You do know how to set a mood, don't you, Dan?"

"Well, thanks."

I wasn't really paying him a compliment.

"Do you read everybody this well?" I asked.

"I don't know what you mean."

Slowly, slowly, he was retracting his embrace.

"I mean, you seem to have a gift for giving people what they need. Especially women." That was no compliment, either, and this time he caught on.

He waited for a few seconds and then repeated in exactly the same tone: "I don't know what you mean."

"You know, Dan, when I met you that day at Stephens, my father told me how good you were at your job. How all the kids liked and respected you. I made a quick judgment about you, but then I realized how unfair I was being."

"What judgment?"

"That you were a compulsive good guy. That you had to make people like you at any cost. You have to be the perfect cool grown-up for the kids. You have to be the perfect employee and son substitute and extra man at the dinner table for my dad. You have to be the perfect liberated husband, the perfect lover for a kook like me."

"Well, I'm just a beautiful human being," he said.

"No, don't get me wrong. I'm not attacking you for trying to be Mister Wonderful."

"What are you attacking me for?"

"Look, the thing is, when you're all things to all people, who are you, really?"

His face went tight. "This is your roundabout way of telling me I'm a phony asshole. Is that it?"

"You're right, I am beating around the bush. Are you a phony? Who knows? The word I really mean is *liar*."

It was a relief, actually, when his temper flared for the first time.

"Enough of this shit, lady. Why don't you just tell me what you're talking about?"

I faced him squarely. "You. Felice. Sanders."

It was fairly dark out on the deck, just the candles for light. I couldn't say for sure that his face was burning, but what I could see was the trapped expression in his eyes.

"Y'all did it, didn't you? You lied to me, didn't you?"

He reached for his wineglass. Well, that sealed it. Guilty as charged.

He heaved an ugly grunt. "My, my. Look who's turning puritan. I thought you were a sophisticated black woman. What about all your dirty encounters all over the globe? Or was that just posturing bullshit?"

"I don't even want to hear that. This is not about how many women you've been with, and you know it."

"What is it about then—Felice being half my age? Are you that provincial?"

"No! And stop stalling! What this is about—as you very well know—is Felice being a kid—a student of yours, or a patient, or whatever you want to call it—but a kid who was all messed up. And you knew it and you slept with her and you lied about it."

No reply to that. He just sucked his top lip under his front teeth.

"Tell me, Dan. Please. She could be in real danger now. The police are involved. Just tell me."

He looked at me, exasperated, angry, and afraid.

"Please!" I said, feeling those same things. "I don't care what you and Felice did together. And I wouldn't even think about telling my father. Ever."

"All right. But first I want it to be clear, I don't know where she is. I didn't do anything to harm her and I do not know where she is now."

I nodded. "Go on."

"There's a place," he began. "An apartment where—Ah, shit, you know what kind of kids go to Stephens. Worldly. Bright. Precocious. A lot of them from money. A lot of them with parents who don't look out for them the way they should. One of the boys has folks who spend half the year in Europe, so he lives with relatives. But he has the key to the parents' apartment in the Village. Sometimes—I—some of the students, the older kids—go there once in a while."

Ah. A house to play house in. Every teenager's dream. No groping at the movies for my pop's students.

"And you," I said, "you went there once in a while, too. With Felice."

He knocked back the remaining wine in his glass and then refilled it. "I know it wasn't the smart thing to do. And I regretted it."

"How often?"

"Two—three, maybe four times."

"Fair amount of regretting. Before or after Black Hat died?"

He clammed up.

"Come on, Dan. You may as well tell me. The truth's out now."

"A few times after, in that apartment. A few times before, not in the apartment."

"Where then? Did you bring her here for the funky cheese and moonlight treatment?"

"No, of course not. It was—"

"Where?"

"At school. At school, okay?"

"Oh Christ. While you were tutoring her for the SATs, right?"

"Fuck you, Nan. That isn't fair."

"I'm sorry. Go on."

"There isn't much more to tell. I lied about sleeping with her, but not about anything else. She was depressed and needy. We'd had a couple of nice times together while she was at Stephens; it wasn't a serious thing for me and it wasn't a serious thing for her. It was just . . . just . . . sex."

I rolled my eyes.

"Look, it's a complicated thing when you deal with young people. Especially smart, good-looking ones. They're looking for approval, looking to seduce you, looking for a father—"

"Forget that, man. Just get on with it."

"All right. After Black Hat died, she was lonely and wanted to be close that way again. Just to be comforted. Grief sex, it's a real thing. Why can't you understand that?"

"When was the last time? When did you last see her?"

"Maybe three weeks ago?"

"But you spoke after that."

"Yes. She called me and she was so off-the-wall I tried to get her to meet me for coffee or something—just so I could calm her down, try to get her to a shrink maybe. But it was no good. She hung up without even telling me where she was living. All she said was that she had an older man in her life and things weren't going well. She said she thought she could trust him when she first met him, but even he had let her down."

I shook my head. Dan must've thought it was just more censure from me. And it was, but I was also trying to clear my head, comb through the tangled threads of lies and double-talk—Dan's, Dr. Benson's, Mrs. Benson's, Ida Williams's—the whole cast of characters.

But then, that was nothing like the whole cast. It was only a partial listing of the credits.

"Are you listening to me at all, Nan?"

"What?"

"I said, I don't care what you think about the stupid thing with Felice—I mean, I do care, but that's not the important thing now. I want you to believe that I haven't been bullshitting you, playing with you. Or your father. I like and respect Eddie. And I want a chance to be with you. Can you hear that?"

"Yeah. Fine. But you've got it wrong. That's not the important thing now. The important thing is getting over to that apartment."

"What? What are you talking about? Now?"

"Yes. Now."

"But why? What do you want to go there for? What difference—"

"I don't want to get into all that now. Maybe I should have told you from the very beginning what the deal was with trying to find Felice Sanders—how I happened to be looking for her. See, I'm no stranger to lying, either. I do it constantly, damn me. But there's lying—and there's lying. Anyway, forget that for now. How do I get in there? Into that knocking shop, as the English would call it."

He winced. "I'd have to call Rob MacLachlin *at home*. He's the student whose parents' place it is."

"Do it."

"But I'd have to— I mean, suppose his— It might get him into trouble."

"Yeah. He's going to think you're really uncool. Call him."

He walked inside and over to the telephone, dragging like a prisoner in leg irons. I watched him as he rustled through the pages of his phone book and then picked up the receiver.

There was some toadying exchange with what I took to be the kid's guardian, a pause, and then Dan began to talk to the boy himself in hushed, urgent tones:

"Rob, listen, it's Dan Hinton . . . Yeah, good . . . Look, about the loft . . . No, forget about that . . . I know. . . . You lent the key to Felice Sanders sometimes, and gave her the code to the street door . . . Never mind that now . . . Just listen. The last time she was up there, I had to go up and talk to her. I left some important papers behind and I've got to have them. I have to have them now, understand? You've got to get me the key. I have to have that key."

His hand cupped over the mouthpiece, he began to relay what Rob MacLachlin was saying to him:

"He's scared. He says he can't give the key to anybody. Some neighbors phoned his aunt and uncle reporting that they've seen a young girl and other people coming and going in the building. One of them was an older black man. Could they be using the MacLachlins' apartment? He guesses it might be Felice they described. But he doesn't understand how that could be. He stopped letting kids use the place months ago."

"Tell him he doesn't know what scared is. Threaten him a little, Dan."

I spat those commands out, very sure of myself, but to be honest I had gone a little numb in the head. Felice had an old black gentleman caller. What was the deal with that? There were two older black men floating around in this mess—Jacob Benson and the man from Ida's past, Miller. Three, if you counted my father. Which I didn't—couldn't.

But I couldn't put either Benson or Miller with Felice. Not only was the good doctor the aged father of her dead boyfriend, it sounded like he and Felice hated each other. And as for Ida's ex-partner, Miller—he and Felice Sanders fit together like I'd fit at a Hells Angels barbecue.

Something else was bothering me. Dan had told me earlier about an older man, but he never said he was black. Why hadn't he supplied that detail? Maybe because Felice had never mentioned the man's color. I didn't know. Anyway, the main thing now was to get into that apartment.

Dan gave me a gruesome smile, hand still over the mouthpiece. "Okay. It's on."

THE TAXI FARE FROM Brooklyn Heights to Beekman Place was steep indeed. Out of guilt, no doubt, Dan refused to let me pay my half.

Young Rob MacLachlin, a towhead on the beefy side, was waiting for us on the street. God knows what he told Auntie and Uncle to get out of the apartment. Very likely he'd thought up a Nanette-size whopper to accomplish it.

I stepped aside to give Dan and the kid a minute's privacy. I don't know which of them looked more abashed. The boy soon handed over the key along with a slip of paper, and we left him standing on the sidewalk.

The MacLachlin place was on Greenwich Street—not busy, touristy Greenwich Avenue, but Greenwich Street, two short blocks from the waterfront—in a renovated manufacturing loft building.

Dan consulted the slip of paper in his hand and then tapped in the numbers for the code box on the street door. We caught the elevator and went up to seven.

All the New York film people were down in the far West Village/Tribeca nabe now, driving already high prices up into the stratosphere. Here and there on the streets were limos with big-shouldered drivers snoozing behind the wheel.

Even while he turned the key in the lock, Dan was still protesting my strong-arm methods, and our whole mission, which he thought was stupid. I shushed him violently and pushed him through the door.

The MacLachlins had the kind of apartment most of us Manhattanites can only dream of. Endless space and skylights and peace and quiet; a brief walk away from the Hudson; and a bevy of cutting-edge, if budget-busting, restaurants just around the corner.

I called out a timid hello. No answer.

But there was a big purple tote bag in the middle of the floor. It was overflowing with clothes: jeans, T-shirts, filmy blouses, leg warmers, and leotards.

"Do they look like they might belong to Felice?" I asked.

He seemed transfixed by the bag. But at last he nodded yes.

"I don't understand," he mumbled.

"Understand what?"

"Rob took the key back. He swore."

"He was telling the truth, most likely. How hard would it be for Felice to have made a key without telling him? She knows the downstairs code, doesn't she?"

"Yeah. That makes sense."

"You check the bedrooms," I said. "I guess you know right where they are."

He gave me a dirty look and headed off down the corridor. I turned into the kitchen area. Everywhere you looked, there was a bowl, a knife, a Dutch oven for every cook I knew to worship and covet. And the wicker hamper outside the door of a small adjoining room was the clue that the MacLachlins had their own laundry room. I just knew there'd be a gleaming washer-dryer combo, one atop the other, that would make me do some worshipping and coveting of my own.

Don't open that door.

That just popped into my head, that command.

But I had to. I had to open it.

I didn't scream. I know I didn't. But the sound I let out was obviously loud enough for Dan to hear it all the way down the hall.

He came running.

The girl was wedged between the appliances and a folding

table. Slumped and staring, almost as if she'd been waiting a long time to be freed, and finally gave up hope.

Then the odor came creeping out. I covered my nose and mouth with my hand, stepped aside just long enough for Dan to get a look.

He sobbed, once.

"So it is her," I said, and closed the door. "No question it's Felice?"

"No."

"Okay," I said quietly, "let me take a quick look around the place. And then we've got to get out of here. Anything out of order in the bedrooms?"

A shake of his head.

"Right. You didn't touch anything, did you?"

Another shake.

"That thing you told your student, whatshisname—you didn't really leave anything here, did you?"

"No."

I did a fast tour of the rest of the loft, using a paper towel when opening and closing cabinet doors, shower curtains, wardrobes. "All right. I guess that's it," I said.

"What are you going to do?"

"Call the police. What do you think?"

"You—you can't . . ." Dan's eyes looked all out of focus. No need to wonder why: he was seeing his career, his life, swimming out to sea, away from him.

"Take it easy. I won't call from inside the apartment. We're getting out of here now. But I have to notify somebody I know in the department."

"You have friends in the department?"

"That doesn't matter now, Dan. Let's go."

I took a precautionary look down at the street, on the chance someone might be on the way up.

We both watched the lighted panel above our heads that chimed out the floors as we descended.

"Okay, Dan. As far as I'm concerned, you don't figure in this thing at all, not tonight, anyway. But the worst is yet to come. You know that, right?"

"I know."

He looked every bit as tragically sorry as he should have been. Every bit as frightened.

We bypassed the public phones of prosperous, fashionable Tribeca, and didn't stop to call Leman Sweet until we were safely on a down-and-out corner of Canal Street. I told Sweet everything about Greenwich Street, everything but the fact of my companion. He told me to put as much space between the loft and myself as humanly possible, for the time being.

I repeated the same advice to Dan. "Go home now. The shit's gonna hit soon enough. Just go home."

"No," he said quietly. "I can't just leave you holding the bag."

"I'm not holding anything, really. I'll be fine."

I couldn't figure out why my words should set him off, but suddenly he was fuming. "Oh, aren't you brave," he said, sneering. "Don't lie to me, Nan. You're just trying to get rid of me so you can go off and do something tough and foolhardy. You're sending cowardly old Mr. Hinton home to shiver in his apartment while you go out and do some macho shit. You go out and solve a murder with your *friends* in the NYPD while I drink my milk and go to bed. Think how well that's gonna play with your papa."

Oh dear. We had a mortally wounded male ego to deal with, on top of everything else.

"You're really into self-flagellation, aren't you, Hinton? Okay, then. I'll call you a pussy. All right? Feel better now?"

Once again my dirty mouth stopped him in his tracks.

"Oh God," he moaned suddenly, bringing his hands up over his face. "Oh God, Nan."

"What? What is it?"

"I want to be with you so bad. Couldn't you come back to my place?"

"*What!*"

"I can't help it, I'm sorry. I'm about to lose everything—everything. My life is over. I need—"

"You need to get your ass on the subway."

I know I sounded mean, but I didn't feel any enmity toward him. Far from it. I did pity him. Insane satyr that he was.

"Where are you going now?" he asked.

"To Caesar's," I told him wearily. "I'll wait there for Leman to tell me what comes next. Now, will you please go."

He shook his head. "Not yet. I have someplace else I have to go."

"Where?"

"To see Rob MacLachlin. He's going to need me."

CHAPTER 15

CLOSE YOUR EYES

THE AFTER-WORK CROWD was gone and the all-nighters had not yet arrived. I had rarely seen the Go Go Emporium so sparsely populated.

Thank God, I saw her right away. There was Aubrey at the end of the bar, pouring orange juice into one of the false-bottom tankards they used to serve draft beer.

She grabbed hold of me. "Nan, what's wrong? You look kinda crazy."

I brought her up to date, smoking furiously as I told the story. I was taking cigarettes from a pack someone had abandoned on the bar along with a set of keys and a pair of eyeglasses.

"Shit," she commented when my narrative ended. "Here we go again."

And didn't that say it all.

I ordered a Jack Daniel's from the bartender, a white guy named Larry whom I had met a few times in the past. He was a decent sort, a pretty obliging fellow, especially when you needed a handful of amphetamines or a color TV for cheap. In fact, Larry, like my friend Patrice, had once arranged for me to buy a gun. That one ended up in the hands of a man who had even less business toting it around than I did.

He greeted me as he set down the double JD, waving away my ten-dollar bill. "Hey, Nanette. How's it going?"

I merely shook my head in answer.

"Yeah, I hear that," he said, and moved away.

Aubrey said, "So that girl is dead."

"Yeah. Dead as can be. Oh Lord, girl."

"Leman going to keep you out of this mess?"

"I don't know. I don't see how he can—now. Maybe the best I can hope for is that Loveless, that Homicide cop, won't push for the death penalty."

"For the one who murdered her, you mean. Or the one who killed Ida."

"No. For me."

"Fuck him. He shoulda listened to you in the first place. And old jughead Leman better look out for you, if he know what's good for him. Don't worry about it."

She began to tunnel into her handbag. "Here. Take some of these."

"What is all that?"

"This one's echinacea," she said, filling a dropper from a big brown bottle. "It tastes pretty nasty, but it keeps you calm. And these are vitamin C. And these here are your complex Bs."

"Oh, come on, please, Aubrey. Don't make me take that shit."

"Go ahead, Nanette. You can use all the help you can get."

I popped the vile pills indiscriminately and started dribbling the viscous brown liquid into my bourbon. But I stopped suddenly.

"Finish it!"

"Okay, okay. Just a second. You just reminded me of something."

"What?"

"Justin."

"What about him?"

"You said I could use all the help I could get. That's what J said when he gave me the Mama Lou doll. Remember? Where is he, anyway?" I asked.

"That's a good question. He didn't show for work today."

"He what?"

"You heard me, he didn't show. They been calling his place since this afternoon, Larry said. There's no answer."

I started to go cold. Lately anything out of the ordinary made me nervous. Lately it seemed that anything could happen to anybody.

Justin was, without making it sound too too dramatic, missing. Felice Sanders was missing, for a while, and now we knew she was not coming back—ever.

"Where do you think he could be?" I asked. "Does Larry have any idea?"

She shrugged. "Hungover, probably. Maybe laying up with somebody. But he's never even ten minutes late getting to work. I don't know—I guess it's kind of weird that he wouldn't—"

"I don't like this," I said, and the phrase turned into a kind of incantation. "I don't like this I don't like this I don't like this."

Aubrey started to laugh, but then she quickly caught on that it was no joke. "What are you acting like that for? You think something happened to him?"

"I'm not sure," I said. "Maybe it's just thinking about Felice that's got me so jumpy. But I need to know he's all right. You know Kenny, Justin's guy?"

"A little."

"Have you got his phone number?"

"No. But it's probably in the book."

"Do me a favor, Aub. Look it up for me, would you?"

Kenny, at least, was at home. He picked up the phone. But the minute I heard his voice, I knew something was amiss.

"Is J with you?" I asked as soon as I had identified myself.

"No," he said, voice tremulous. "That's just the trouble."

"What trouble?"

"He's not here, he's not at home, and I know he's not at work because I've been calling him there for hours. I can't find him anywhere. I'm getting worried, Nan."

"I know. I know. Do you have his keys by any chance?"

"No. I've got a bad feeling. What should we do?"

"For the moment, nothing. Sit tight, Kenny. I'll call you back as soon as—"

I looked up then. Aubrey was hovering over me. Her expression kept changing from confusion to panic and back again.

"I'll be in touch, Kenny," I said, and hung up.

"Where is he at, Nan!" she demanded. "What happened to J?"

I reached for another cigarette.

Here we go again.

We talked one of the bouncers into going over to Justin's apartment to check it out. He came back with a report that the super had gone inside J's place and found no one at home and nothing disturbed.

On the off chance that he had called me, I phoned my apartment and retrieved my messages. Nothing.

We hung in at Caesar's for another couple of hours, hoping foolishly that Justin would show up with a rational explanation for his disappearance—at least hoping to hear from him. But even as I hoped, and drank, and smoked, I knew it was no go.

I went home about two in the morning feeling like a windup clock that was just about to pop a spring. There had been a call from Sweet telling me that the police were all over the Greenwich Street loft and that Rob MacLachlin's parents had been contacted in Geneva. Sweet had fed the higher-ups a story about an anonymous tip on the scene at the loft. He wanted me to call him in the morning for further updates.

Yes, I'd surely be doing that. But if Justin didn't surface by morning, I'd have to throw myself on Sweet's mercy and ask him for help in finding J, too. And that would mean I'd have to come clean about J's involvement in the break-in at Ida's.

Here we go again: that fearful symmetry. Two dolls. Two elderly black men. Two apartment break-ins. Two missing persons, one of them no longer missing, and one whose happiness and safety I'd jeopardized by pulling him in on my investigation.

I snatched one of the dolls off the desk—Dilsey—and paced around with her for a while, staring into her face as if awaiting enlightenment. She never gave it up, though. Her fierce expression never changed.

Finally, tired beyond the telling, I fell onto the couch and tried to sleep. No luck with that, either.

I turned on the radio and got one of the night-owl stations that played American pop standards throughout the night. Some Vegas tenor's fatuous version of the great "Laura." A medley by the often ill-used Jo Stafford. And then the Ray Conniff Singers applying themselves to "Dontcha Go 'Way Mad."

I sat up suddenly in the darkness.

While I was cadging those cigarettes at the bar at Caesar's, my hand kept hitting the eyeglasses lying next to the pack.

Get some new glasses.

Or something like that. That creep Lyle had said something like that to Kenny.

I swiped the phone off the hook and dialed Kenny's number again. Like I figured, he wasn't sleeping.

"Justin?" he called desperately into the receiver.

"No, Kenny. It's me, Nan. Listen to me. I know you're going nuts worrying about J. But something else is wrong, too, isn't it?"

He didn't say anything for a moment. "Well . . ."

"Go ahead, Kenny. Tell me."

"I didn't want to say anything to you. I guess I was too ashamed. But I got . . . bashed. Last night. Some bastard jumped me. Right in front of my apartment building. If there hadn't been a crowd of people coming out of a party across the street, that son of a bitch might've beat me to death. I really think that's what he was trying to do."

Damn. I thought there was something else bothering him when we'd spoken earlier. "Did you see who did it?"

"No. It was dark and he had on a ski mask. But we know who did it: some dickless homophobe."

"You told J about it, right?"

"He came over here after work this morning and found me with a black eye and the world's fattest lip. Left my apartment early today, and I haven't seen him since."

There it was. I knew with absolute certainty then that Justin wasn't off "laying up" with anybody. I knew where Justin was.

In one movement, it seemed, I had my shoes on—and was checking the load in my Beretta and grabbing my coat and scraping the keys off the kitchen table.

What were the chances I'd be mugged or arrested for soliciting if I ran downstairs now and tried to get a cab?

I had to risk it.

THE SECURITY GUARD banged heavily on the door to Lyle Corwin's office.

"Open it! Just open it!" I shouted.

He fumbled for the key, found it, and unlocked the door. I rushed past him.

Justin, kind of like Aubrey, was always conscious of the things that differentiated "classy" people from the rest of us. Rich people, he said, judged you by your footwear. He loved to buy beautiful, expensive socks.

Tonight he had on his gray-and-white Paul Smith numbers.

He was lying near the desk, not moving. His face was covered with blood.

I fell to my knees, already half blind with tears.

I picked up his hand. How I wanted to talk to him. "Oh, friend . . . oh, friend," I wailed.

It all went rushing by my eyes—calling Aubrey to tell her the worst had happened, hearing her anguished cry. How she would blame me for it all, and rightly so. How Leman Sweet would curse me. How Loveless would lock me up for withholding evidence. How Dan would lose his job. How Pop would revile me.

I wept horribly, so pitifully that the guard reached down and tried to comfort me with his arms.

Then we heard a whistling sound emanate from beside the desk. I was so startled that I let J's hand flop back down on the floor.

He was breathing!

Breathing heavily through the blood in his nostrils. He'd lost a front tooth, so there was blood in his mouth as well.

"Get help!" I screamed. The guard took off.

I leaned over Justin, called his name.

He cried out in pain then, and clutched his side.

"Don't move anymore, okay? Just lie still. Lyle did this to you, didn't he?"

Agitated, he mumbled something I couldn't make out. I understood one thing, though: he wasn't denying what I'd just said.

"All right, all right, honey." I tried to soothe him. "They're coming. The ambulance is on the way."

I heard his very faint "No, don't like hospital."

"Well, that's tough shit, J. You're going."

Now he was crying.

WE HAD TO WAIT in the corridor while they did the paperwork. The doctor was with another patient, they said, and would be out as quickly as he could.

I held J's hand tightly as he lay on the chrome rollaway bed. The feeble Tylenol-ass stuff they'd given him didn't even begin to address the pain, so I bitched until a nurse arrived with a lovely full hypo.

"Is that any better?" I said.

Nodding out. "It's rocking, child."

HE WAS CLEANED UP and taped up and drinking the Starbucks coffee I'd brought him.

"Lyle," he said, "him and that guy."

"Miller," I supplied. "He's the one who hurt you?"

He nodded. "I think so. I was tangling with Lyle when somebody hit me hard from behind. Then I had the two of them to deal with."

"Jesus Christ, J. You had no business going up there like that. All on your own."

"I been going to the gym for a years now, Smash. And plus I surprised him with a wrench." His hand curled around an imaginary weapon and he attempted to lift it.

"You take it easy."

"When somebody beat on Kenny like that," he said, "I said to myself, this is too big a coincidence."

"And you were dead right."

"I just knew that asshole Lyle was behind what happened to

Kenny. The way it happened—the gay-bashing thing just didn't figure. Those animals like to travel in packs and they don't even try to hide their pimply faces. No—I remembered how Lyle told y'all that he didn't know Miller. He knew Kenny didn't believe him."

"So he decided to shut him up," I said. "Kenny did see Lyle talking with Miller at Mary's. There was no mistake."

"Yes. I decided Lyle's ass needed a good kicking. I didn't say anything, but I thought maybe he might even come at you."

"Why me?"

"Because. Because everything seemed so knotted up together. See, I know from Aubrey about you and this cop working on a missing girl case, and how you figure it's tied up with Ida getting killed. And while I was wailing on Lyle—trying to make him tell me the truth about Miller—why was it so important to deny knowing him—the rest of the story started to come out. Some of it, anyway."

"What story?"

"The girl, the girl. The one missing. Lyle knows her."

"Felice Sanders? Are you kidding?"

"Lyle's got a finger in all kinds of penny-ante crap. He's a suck-up to anybody famous who can stand him, and he's a so-called agent and manager to people who think they're gonna be famous but mostly haven't got a shot in hell. The girl contacted him a while back, after some kid she knew died."

"What for?"

"Because he was supposedly 'representing' the kid. She was convinced that all the tapes and videos and whatnot that the kid had made himself were going to be valuable now. Now that he was dead. She wanted Lyle to produce an album. Make the kid a rap star—after his death. You get it?"

He looked as if he was attempting to rise up on one elbow.

"Yeah I get it," I said, pressing his shoulders back down. "Go ahead."

"Lyle knew the kid's music was lame. Nobody was gonna buy that shit. But he didn't tell her that. He drew up some kind of bullshit contract they both signed. Told her she'd have to help finance the deal. He suckered her, see. Took three or four hundred off her—whatever she could raise—and when she couldn't give him any more, he was ready to blow her off. But then he got to thinking: Black Hat's family. The girl was mad at them. But he'd heard they were loaded."

"So he suddenly was very interested in promoting the Black Hat legend."

"I suppose so. I mean, not too long after that, there was regular dough rolling in from Black Hat's people. Even though Lyle hadn't produced a damn thing, and had no intention to."

Huh. I decided not to interrupt J's recitation, but huh? How could that be? Everybody has confirmed that Felice was trying to get money from the Bensons, and was furious with them because they said no.

Justin went on. "Then, several weeks later, this man shows up at Lyle's office. A spiffy-looking old guy."

"Who is black," I said.

"Yeah. A handsome older man. No way it's not Miller, right?"

"Absolutely right."

So much for thinking that Felice could not possibly have been hooked up with Miller. It had to be he who was seen with her at the Greenwich Street loft building.

"We all know how spooked Lyle was when Kenny insisted he and Miller were tight. He was obviously trying to put mucho distance between him and that dude. You and Kenny came up here asking him about Miller. That was bad enough. When I told him the cops were all over this missing-girl thing, he freaked out.

Now it was gonna look like he was in on kidnapping her—or whatever it is happened to her."

I'd wait a little bit longer, I decided, before telling him the truth about Felice.

"That's when Miller walked in. I don't know what he hit me with, but I swear I thought I'd had it. I couldn't get much of a close look at him. Only for a moment when he and Lyle were grabbing things out of the desk. Then I passed out. You know they must be on the run now."

"They better keep running," I said. "Him and Lyle."

"No, don't. Don't try to go after them," he pleaded, and winced with the effort. "You'll get hurt. And don't tell Aubrey and them at Caesar's, either. Lot of people'll end up dead. Please don't, Nan. Promise."

But before I could agree to do as he asked, the white coats were shuffling me out of his room.

CHAPTER 16

WE SEE

MUCH AS I WOULD HAVE LIKED to see some of the gorillas from Caesar's flay Lyle and Miller alive, I was honoring Justin's request for now. Besides, I was loath to tell Aubrey that Justin's battered condition was all my fault. I'd have to work my way up to that. But at least I was able to set her mind at ease about J's whereabouts. As to how he came to be lying in a hospital bed, I handed her one of my Pulitzer Prize–winning lies.

This one had Justin drinking with friends in a West Side bar that was invaded by two particularly brutal hold-up men. By the time she pulled apart all the inconsistencies, she'd be in a cab with a two-pound box of chocolates and an armload of dahlias for his bedside table.

And by the time she cross-checked my story with the story that Justin would no doubt come up with, and tried to get me on the phone, I'd be out of the house.

But for now, I was eating my breakfast—replete with hot biscuits and real sliced country ham and buttered grits—a takeout order from the faux soul food place I'd raided on my way home from the hospital. It would be the last time for quite a while that I'd sit calmly, thoughtfully, in my own kitchen, at least half-way peaceful with myself. But of course I didn't know it at that moment.

I gave myself time that morning, after breakfast, to pick up around the apartment and find a place for every utensil and stray dishcloth and coffee cup in the kitchen, to take a long bath and listen to Ravel and bundle up the old catalogs, and do every kind of normal household chore I'd neglected.

I had the time, for instance, to regret the way things had gone with Dan Hinton. But he'd told me too many lies. It's always galling to realize that a guy has lied to you. Plainly, none of the men in this case was any prize in the honesty department.

Working my way backward and forward through the big fat braid of events, it occurred to me that just about *every guy* I'd encountered lately had lied to me. Was I being fair in that generalization?

I started a list.

Lyle Corwin—no matter what I promised J, if I ever got the chance, I was going to fix that son of a bitch.

Dan Hinton—need I say more?

My father—jury's still out on that one.

Miller—the dark prince—even at age sixty-something he must be quite a man—a dangerous, world-class liar, no question in my mind.

Rob MacLachlin—lied to parents and guardians—maybe more of his lies to be uncovered—I didn't predict a happy adult-hood for the boy.

Dr. Benson—lied—lied about wife and pretty obviously lied about his lack of ill will toward Felice Sanders—clearly he had not wanted Black Hat to marry "the girl."

Black Hat/Kevin—big question mark—the poor baby had

died so young, he probably hadn't had the opportunity to become a practiced liar—on the face of it, anyway, he was the only male with clean hands and no ulterior motives.

Leman Sweet—certainly could lie/would lie without blinking if it suited his purposes—but to be honest, all the lies in our relationship had come from my end—he might detest me, but so far he had been straight with me.

Loveless, the Bad Lieutenant—arrogant bastard—thought so much of himself he probably felt no need to lie—but maybe he was being less than forthright with Leman Sweet about the progress of the case.

Justin—well, perhaps I ought to withhold judgment on him. A major drama queen, true, capable of gross exaggeration. But hadn't he just passed the truth-and-loyalty test, getting stomped in the process?

Kenny—see Justin, above.

Lefty, the ponytailed lock picker—Lord have mercy, there was somebody running the streets of New York City who actually thought my name was Thelma. Justin had helped him out of a situation that might have landed him in prison virtually for life. Sounded like lying was one of the nicer things he did.

I was leaving somebody out of the litany. Who?

Everything took me back to the beginning of the story—to the dolls, to Ida.

Who had set me on the path to the real Ida Williams? Who was it that set my break-in of Alice Rose's lovely apartment into motion?

Another man. Another liar.

He had checked out my bod in the all-black getup I was wearing. Flirted with me, flattered me outrageously. I had his phone number in the back pocket of those black jeans, didn't I?

Funny. You do not *look like a Howard.*

CHAPTER 17

ASK ME NOW

WALK UP TO HIM on the street. Put the barrel of the gun in his ear and give him five seconds to talk.

Not too subtle.

Hide myself in the bushes with the squirrels, watch him until he knocks off work, and then follow him, wherever that might take me.

Squirrels are rodents, aren't they? Think again.

It was late afternoon by the time I arrived in Union Square Park. I found a bench near the children's play area, facing Broadway. Through the thin stream of traffic I could see him at his table.

Howard was doing pretty good business. Several people stopped to buy his bargain-priced art books over the course of the two hours I sat quietly with my giant-size container of coffee and the newspaper I was using as camouflage.

Around five-thirty, the sunlight all gone now, he started boxing up the unsold books. I walked over there.

I dropped my voice way down—Kathleen Turner with a cold: "Did you think I lost your number?"

He looked up from his packing. "You," he said simply. If I was reading it right, he was glad to see me.

I let him get a good look. "Am I too early for dinner?"

"You're right on time. But I'm not dressed."

"Yeah you are. I'd notice if you weren't."

"I mean not dressed to take you out."

"You're fine. I thought we could go casual. Grab a burger and a drink around the corner at the Old Town. We'll make an early night of it. Dessert at my place—if that's all right with you."

"That is all kinds of all right with me. I don't have any flowers and candy. How about a book for you? You like Magritte?"

"I do."

He hefted the oversized volume and presented it to me.

"You like Jacob Lawrence?"

"Of course."

I stopped him before he gave me that one as well.

"Why don't we keep them in the box for now?" I suggested. "We'll put them on my coffee table later."

I waited while he stowed the cartons in the back of his worn station wagon and locked up.

The Old Town was aptly named. Unlike Pete's Tavern, only a block east, or staid old Fraunces Tavern, it did not claim to be the oldest bar in Manhattan. But it had been serving up hamburgers and spirits to generations of New Yorkers since the late nineteenth century.

The usual mix of college students, neighborhood people, tourists, and solid elderly drunks mingled at the curlicued dark wood bar up front. A small, underlit room at the rear had a scattering of tables for smokers. And there was a kind of annex upstairs, a quite large dining room, actually. But I had seen it only a couple of times when I'd walked up there to use the toilet. I didn't want to deal with any stairs today.

We arrived a few minutes before six, just ahead of the thirsty after-office-hours crowd. We were able to capture one of the coveted booths near the front. These had narrow seats and high backs. How lovely. We'd be nice and private.

"Don't sit there," I said playfully when Howard began to slide onto the seat opposite mine. "Come over here—next to me."

He ordered a Guinness stout (which I'd always thought of as drinking a cigar) along with a shot of some upscale single malt. I stayed with my usual JD, limiting myself to one and then switching to mineral water. A while later we ordered food. The burgers were pretty tasty and mine came with a ton of good, garlicky potato salad. Howard was getting a nice buzz on, which didn't dull his flirtatious patter one bit. He fed me french fries from his plate and spoke to me with his lips close to my ear.

I would soon have to switch gears on him.

"By the way, did I ever thank you?" I said.

"For the books? You can thank me later. At your place."

"No, not the books. For giving me that information about Ida Williams. You know, that first day I met you."

"Oh. That's okay."

"It was very helpful—the thing about Alice Rose and the apartment uptown."

He nodded. "Good. Let's get another round."

"Sure," I said.

"Guinness and a Jack," he called to the waitress who was flying by the table at that moment. "You've had enough of that water, haven't you, Nan?"

"Okay, one more Jack," I said, and then picked up where I'd left off. "There's just one thing I can't thank you for, Howard."

He didn't ask what that thing was. Clearly, he didn't want to know.

I told him, anyway: "You neglected to tell me about the rest of your business with Ida—or Alice—or whatever her name was. And you didn't mention one word about Miller."

"Miller?" he repeated, suddenly belligerent.

"Did you order a Miller?" That was the waitress, as she set down our drinks.

"No, this is cool," Howard said, dismissing her. He turned back to me then. "Who's Miller?"

"That's my line, Howie. I was hoping you could tell me exactly who he is. And what he and Ida Williams were all about."

He began shaking his head. "Look, I did you a favor, okay. You asked me about Ida and I told you. I dropped a sewing machine off at her place and it was a different name on the bell. That's all I know."

He whipped his head around, away from me, startled to see the press of people with their backs to us. Dozens of them. In the time we had been sitting there, the bar had filled to capacity and folks were standing three abreast at the bar.

"What are you getting so upset about, Howard? Looking for the waitress? Don't ask for the check yet, baby. We're not ready to leave."

"Maybe you not ready, but I am."

"Oh, come on. Don't move away from me like that. Stay close."

"Forget you."

"No, honest, I mean it," I said. "Stay close. Look down here—on your thigh. Or did you think that was my hand?"

He went rigid, staring down at the gun. The filthy words began to leak from his mouth, though I didn't know how, because I could swear his lips never moved.

"Yeah, I know," I said. "It does seem excessive, doesn't it? But look at it this way: you're paying for the sins of all men—all the men I been meeting lately, anyway. And to tell you the truth, Howard, I'm tired of being lied to by you assholes. Damn tired. So let's have the Ida Williams story. Now."

I poked him gently with the muzzle. For emphasis.

I thought for a minute there I'd have to peel him off the ceiling.

"Be careful with that motherfu—"

"Not to worry, I took lessons. You go on and drink your beer while we talk."

He picked up the glass and took a good pull.

"First of all, you told me when we met that Ida worked the Union Square market more or less every other day. I need to know what she did with herself when she wasn't down here."

"How should I know that?"

"Come on, Howard," I said, poking him with the gun. "What was it you said to me? Think about it—hard."

"She sold her stuff uptown. At a street market a lot like ours. It's on First Avenue."

"Fine. Did Ida have a buyer for her dolls up there—a rich black woman, very refined, who lives up around the hospitals?"

"I don't—"

I dug the muzzle deeper into his lap.

"Okay, just give me a chance to answer, okay!"

"Go on."

"Maybe she was a customer and maybe not, but Ida was hanging out with a woman like that—a lot."

"Was there a man with them? About Ida's age?"

"Usually not. But I did see him once or twice."

"What were they doing?"

Here he became less than forthcoming. He looked searchingly at the crowd of patrons, all of whom had their backs to us. Maybe he was desperately calculating the odds of making it safely through the tangle of people and out the front door before I could catch up with him. He didn't have a chance in hell and he knew it.

"Noisy in here, isn't it?" I noted. "I guess you didn't hear my last question. I asked what they were doing."

"All right, listen, you crazy— Just listen. My next sentence is going to begin with the words *I don't know.* But that's just the *start* of what I'm about to tell you, understand? Just let me finish what the fuck I'm trying to say before you jam that thing into my balls again. Okay?"

"Yes."

"Okay. I don't know what they were doing. All I did was pick up or deliver stuff for them. Sometimes Ida sends me to the Lower East Side for the cloth she sews with. Sometimes I'd drive her rich friend back home."

"Back from where?"

"Either one of the coffee shops in the Village or the room near the piers."

"The piers on the Hudson River? You mean along West Street? Those piers?"

"Yeah. Crystal Meth Avenue. Blow Job Boulevard."

"And what room are you talking about?"

"In one of the skanky apartment hotels. There's dozens of them fronting on the river. The boys take their tricks there. Or the tricks take their boys there. Whatever. Hasn't that been going on for the last fifty years or something?"

"I do believe you're right," I said. "Tell me about 'the room.' "

He shrugged. "It's a room. What do you want me to say? Ida and the dude keep a room there. And before you dig that thing into me again, I got no idea why they keep a place there. She's got a nice crib uptown. Maybe the dump is where he lives. I've never actually been inside it."

"What about these innocent deliveries you make? Where do you pick them up from?"

"Sometimes the bank. A few times I met that lady at the bank and then I took an envelope from her and brought it to Ida. And then, sometimes I—"

"Yeah, go on."

"Sometimes I score for them."

"Score." I cleared my throat. "You're saying you cop for them? Ida and Miss Lady."

"Nothing too heavy. Pills. Acid. Ida had me score that a few times."

"You're putting me on."

"No."

"Ida and the rich lady are tripping balls in a ratty hotel room on West Street. You think I believe that? Maybe you think I'm the one who's tripping?"

"Look, you asked. I told you."

I frowned. Not just because I didn't believe it. More because it represented yet another complication. A ridiculous one.

I groaned then, and must have inadvertently shoved the gun farther in, because he yelped "Hey!" loudly enough to cause a few people to turn and look our way.

The harried waitress assumed Howard was rudely summoning her. She walked briskly over to the table and threw down our check, turned on her heel and left.

"Let's go," I said decisively, throwing a few tens on the table.

He looked at me, incredulous. "*Go?* Where the hell do you think I'm gonna go with you?"

"Up and out, sweetie."

We looked like a couple in love. Entwined. Certainly I must've looked eager—a girl who couldn't keep her hands off her man.

We walked out of the restaurant, turned left, then right on

Park, and cut through the now-empty farmers market, found his station wagon on Seventeenth.

Howard kept his eyes on the road for most of the short trip west. The balance of the time he was looking down at the gun and where it was aimed.

He muttered something.

"What was that?"

"I said I was just making extra coin. I never did anything illegal. You just try to prove that I did."

"I don't think that'll be necessary." No, you didn't do nothing illegal. Buying street drugs is no different than picking up a half dozen eggs. "Just answer a few more questions and this date'll be history. By the way, have you got any idea why somebody would want to kill Ida?"

"No, goddammit! I knew you were going to try to put me in that."

"Take it easy, take it easy. Nobody's trying to put you in that. Did it ever look like Ida, or Miller, was forcing this woman into the car? Or forcing her to do anything, for that matter."

"Kind of like kidnapping, you mean. Kind of like what you're doing to me. No. Half the time she looked spaced. But I never saw them hurt her. Like I said, I didn't—"

"Yeah, I know. Nothing illegal. Never asked questions. Extra coin."

It was cold near the water. No people about. Not even the odd hustler in spangles doing curbside business. The air sweeping in off the Hudson had a hint of snow in it. It was dark as hell, too. The darkness seemed so much deeper over here. Not like it was—ordinary, pedestrian friendly—on the well-trafficked streets near safe old Union Square with its stone fountain and Gandhi statue.

We parked, probably illegally, then walked up to the doorway of the no-name hotel, my piece an inch or two from Howard's spine.

"You're sure this is the one?" I said.

After he grunted yes, I reached up to ring the bell on the side of the door frame.

The nanosecond it took me to do that presented Howard with an opportunity he couldn't refuse. He reeled around and swung hard to his right, connecting with my chin. My gun went flying, and with a mighty shove from him, so did I. I landed down in the nasty hollow that had once been the doorway of a basement apartment. When I could sit up again without seeing stars, he was gone.

And so ended our night. It would've been over soon, anyway. Only now I was stranded on this godforsaken spot of concrete. True, it was only a couple of blocks to Hudson Street, where normal street life—including cabs and buses—would be going on. But I wasn't looking forward to traipsing around the piers by myself in the dense night. At least I had a weapon, though. That counted for something.

I scrambled around and found the gun, then picked myself up. My jaw ached something fearsome, but I was in one piece.

I anticipated trouble of some kind from the skinny guy at the front desk. The, uh, concierge, watching a portable TV through his greasy spectacles. No doubt, he expected me to ask for a by-the-hour room and pay in advance. Which I would do—except I wanted a particular room. I wanted the one where Ida and Mrs. Benson, and possibly Miller, hung out.

What I expected was, he'd say that was impossible, because it was a private residence. Then I'd offer him a few bucks just to let me look around in there; he could stand there and watch me if he wanted. I'd touch nothing, I'd take nothing.

He didn't say any of those things, though. Because those tenants, he said, had moved out. The room was open to anybody who wanted to pay for it. So I did.

The place was somebody's version of clean. Thin sheets on a thin mattress. Two windows, each looking out on nothing. Well, at least no corpse in the bathtub. I decided to get out of there before I slit my wrists. Last gesture, I opened the sole drawer in the rickety table on the far wall.

I reached inside and tugged at a piece of paper wedged in the back corner. It wasn't paper; it was a snapshot. Ah. It was a ghost.

It was Black Hat.

No, I shouldn't call him that. I should say instead that I was looking at Kevin, because the sweetly untroubled face of the boy whose photo I was gazing at held nothing of his future as a failed rapper, nor a son who reviled his parents, nor a hapless Romeo deprived of his Juliet, nor a rotting corpse sleeping uneasily, and forever, in the family plot.

On the way out, I thanked the desk guy, and just happened to notice the dark object atop his ancient TV.

"Give you ten bucks for that," I said, pointing at it.

A boy doll. Or do I mean a doll boy. Wearing the cutest little baggy denims and a Chicago Bulls cap. The spitting image of Kevin.

I'll amend that. This time it was altogether appropriate to call him Black Hat.

I hadn't dotted every one of the *i*'s and crossed every one of the *t*'s yet. Not just yet. But I had the feeling that my old friend synchronicity—or was it my nemesis—was going to provide an answer to many riddles.

CHAPTER 18

BLUE ROOM

HAIR PULLED BACK and shining. No jewelry at all. Lenore Benson might have been on the way to one of the endless fund-raisers that women of her class seemed always to be organizing. She was in dark blue cashmere this time. Carolina Herrera, I believe. And the sleeves covered those ugly slashes on her wrists very nicely.

She was composure itself, sitting there in front of the window on that straight-back chair. A few magazines lay at her feet.

I wanted to cry. Not just out of sympathy for all her losses. I could have cried with exhaustion and frustration.

Ida had been murdered. My friend Justin had been beaten to a pulp and his lover had narrowly escaped the same treatment. Dan Hinton's life was in ruins. I had brandished my gun and almost gelded Mr. No Questions Asked—Howard. I'd taken a mean sock in the face at Hotel Sleaze, where anything might have happened to me.

And what did I have to show for it all? A stick-figure likeness of Kevin Benson that Ida must have fashioned for Lenore Benson.

Maybe Ida had been killed before she got the chance to give it to her. Maybe Mrs. Benson had left it in the room by mistake. I didn't know.

The kindly smile on Lenore's lips was a permanent fixture, attached to nothing in reality, I realized, when she looked right through me and said, "I've finished with my tray. You may take it now. Thank you."

I took the chair next to hers. "How are you today, Mrs. Benson?"

"I'm not tired at all, thank you."

"I'm happy to hear that," I said.

I was stuck there, trying to think of a way to communicate with her, to make her hear me, understand me, trust me—frightened I'd say the wrong thing. What if she began to cry? What if she screamed?

Lenore Benson's good manners were her only device for holding the rest of the world at bay. If the Black Hat doll pressed the wrong button, it might just drive her deeper into madness.

I looked over and smiled at the night nurse, who looked coldly back at me.

"I have a little present here, Mrs. Benson. May I give it to you?"

"More oranges, dear? No, thank you. I couldn't eat another bite."

"No, not oranges. I brought you this."

I allowed her to get a good look at the doll, and then handed it to her gently, my movements slow and deliberate. "I thought it might keep you company here, until you can go back home to all your other dolls."

I saw the recognition break onto her face. So far, so good.

Far from tears or hysterics, she was happy. I had made the right decision.

"Oh, thank you, Ida," she said, beaming. "He's looking very well indeed." But then I noticed the puzzlement on her face. "But he won't sing here, will he? You said he'll only sing when we're in the room."

She took in a deep gulp of air. And then Lenore Benson, at the top of her lungs, unloosed the vilest stream of cuss words I had ever heard in my life. That is saying something. I didn't use language like that even when my steam iron exploded in my hand.

The oddest thing of all was the expression on her face: pure delight.

She raised her hands up out of her lap and I leaned away from her, thinking she was about to strike me. But that wasn't it. Still cursing incoherently, she began tapping out an artless beat on the back of my chair. Not a strong beat, but a straight-ahead and soulful one.

My God, she was accompanying herself. She was improvising—rapping!

Said Ernestine: *Close your mouth, girl, before you start catching flies.*

Queen Lenore rapped about my mama. She rapped about *her* mama. Before she was done, she had touched on the crank and the crack and the other kind of crack.

It was a hypnotic performance. After it was over, she returned to her ultra-placid state, the doll cradled in her lap.

I could not take my eyes off of her, but it was definitely time to go. I left there walking backward.

At the elevator bank I ran into Dr. Bergash, Lenore's shrink. He nodded at me. But again, no meeting my eyes.

"I can't help you." Bergash said that to Leman and me on

that first visit to Mrs. Benson. He seemed to be at pains to avoid engaging with us in any way.

Oh . . . okay, Doc. I get it, I thought as I rode down.

LEMAN. I had to talk to Leman Sweet. But I couldn't find the public phones at the clinic.

There was a place on Sixty-ninth Street. An awful bar where I gigged a couple of times last year with a sixties nostalgia band whose regular tenor was in rehab.

It was the only place I could think of in the nabe. So I ran out of the clinic and across York Avenue to that dark, stanky joint, where I'd once seen three mice frolicking on top of the jukebox.

You opened the front door of the place and the smell of stale beer and ancient hamburger grease went up into your sinuses like a swarm of diseased insects. The dark corridor leading to the bar held the unspeakable bathrooms and the phones so old they still had rotary dials. I suppose the occasional drug deal took place there, too.

I dug into the pockets of my jacket. No loose change. I rattled the small shoulder bag that held my gun. None in there, either. I continued on into the bar and asked for a fistful of quarters. And, as long as I was right there, I ordered a bourbon.

Finally the story had come together. I had just about everything put together now. Just about everything but the bodies. Enough drama and violence and star-crossed parallels for a Black History Month miniseries. Can't you just see the image of Mama Lou under the closing credits?

I downed my drink, ordered a second one, and headed with it to the phone.

Sweet picked up immediately.

"My brother," I said in greeting.

"Who the fuck is this? Is that you, Cueball?"

"It's me. I've got things to tell you, buddy. But first I want to hear you say I'm your sister."

I heard his crazed cackle at the other end of the line. "Yeah, that'll be the day."

"Hey," I said harshly, "I'm not one of them, Leman. And I'm glad I'm not."

"One-a who?"

"You know, like the Bensons. And I'm not like you, either. You're pigheaded and mean. But you're still my bro. And I'm sorry I sicced Aubrey on you like that. I used to write poems, did you know that? I just heard some rapping that beats anything I ever set to paper—by the way, do you really like that shit?"

"You oughta be taken off the streets, girl. This stuff is getting to you."

"Tell me something I don't know. Listen, Leman Sweet 'n' Sour. It's busting open. The whole thing."

"I know. I just tried you at Aubrey's. I been calling all over town for you."

"What's happening?"

"I'll start small and then work my way up to the big stuff."

"Start, man, start."

"First, Loveless's people finally tracked down somebody who could tell them what Ida and Miller used to do when they worked in nightclubs."

I piped up: "They made things appear out of nowhere. And sometimes they made things disappear. Illusionists, they're called. Smoke and mirrors and telling the future. And talking to the dead. Psychic scam artists."

There was a long pause. "How did you know that?"

I laughed bitterly. "Felice Sanders told me. Black Hat told me, too."

"Felice Sanders couldn't tell you nothing. Are you drunk, Cueball?"

I thought about it. "Yeah. A little. A drink helps to loosen the grooves, doesn't it? Listen, what about going over the plot of this soap opera I been following, Leman? You like a good story, the way I do?"

"You really are high, ain't you?"

"Just listen for a minute, okay?"

"Okay," he agreed, reluctantly.

"Dr. Benson and his family had a good life, right? Things were cooking for them for a long time. He and his wife must've had some pretty high hopes for their boy Kevin. Just ask me; I know something about mamas' and daddies' high hopes. But then the kid grew up, and the shit hit the fan. Not only did he pick a poor little white girl to marry, he decided he wanted to be a rap niggah called Black Hat. No way were they having that. But then something happened to settle that family feud once and for all. The poor kid got killed—caught a bullet aimed at somebody else. Everybody was fucked up behind that. Everybody. And the wife takes it so bad that she winds up in a posh laughing academy in her Nino Cerruti knits.

"A while later, Ida Williams, a nice old lady who sells dolls on the street, gets popped by a stray bullet. Strange coincidence, isn't it, Sweet?"

"Right. Yeah, it is. Because it turned out that Ida had a connection to Black Hat's family—those crazy dolls that your friend turned you on to."

"Yes. Now, what else happened? Several people overheard Kevin's fiancée, Felice, threaten to take some action that was going to knock the Bensons for a loop. Nobody knew it at the time, but she was trying to get Black Hat's music out, make his name even after he was dead. Too bad for her, the one she turned to for help was this greedy loser Lyle Corwin."

"Biggest mistake that little chick ever made," Leman said.

"I have to agree with you there. Before you know it, Felice goes missing. We don't know what happened to her, but we know it can't be good. Little Nan gets access to the place where Felice has been staying, and sure enough, the worst has already happened. She is dead.

"So here's another weird parallel: my . . . my source, let's call him . . . the one who helped me get into Ida's place, the one who helped me finger Lyle. He goes missing, too. He's bloody, but alive. And before they kick me out of his hospital room, he's able to tell me that Lyle Corwin is somehow hooked up with this man Miller—Ida's cohort, and maybe even Felice's cohort. I mean, there were three older black men weaving in and out this plot—Jacob Benson, Miller—"

"And your old man," Sweet added.

"Yep, my very own father. Anyway, of all of them, Miller seems like the hands-down candidate to be involved with the girl. Benson claimed he had nothing against Felice, but I never bought that. Anybody could tell he detested her. And I know I'm not objective, Sweet, but there's about as much chance of my pop seducing Felice Sanders as me playing a sold-out gig at the Garden.

"So what do we have? Everybody's tied up with everybody else. Including yours truly. Everybody's suffering over their losses and trying in whatever way they can to get back what they've lost—or to get even. I'm telling you, Sweet, when you pick through all the strands, the answer is right there. So simple."

"Simple? You mean you know what it's all about—who did what to who? Go ahead, give me the word."

"Okay. Like I said, it's simple. Well, maybe not that simple. Maybe not simple at all. But so sad. Sad enough to make you start drinking."

"You done enough of that for one night, Cueball. I'm coming to get you. Where are you calling from?"

I was about to answer that question, but we were cut off.

No, Ma Bell didn't disconnect us. Nor did Sweet hang up on me. Jacob Benson had reached over my shoulder and broken the connection.

He had his own gun, too.

The last thing I saw as Dr. Benson propelled me away from the telephone was a cockroach scrambling for cover.

CHAPTER 19

AS LONG AS I LIVE

HE FLUNG LITTLE BLACK HAT into the nearest sidewalk trash bin.

"What kind of black monster are you, bringing her that god-damn thing? You like seeing her misery, don't you? Even after she's got nothing left, you people are still trying to suck her blood. You won't be satisfied until she's dead!"

His raw whisper was like a lash across the back.

I wanted to speak. He didn't even try to hear me.

"Say nothing," he warned. "I'd just as soon kill you right here. Do you understand?"

What did he want me to do? Which was it? Keep silent or say that I understood?

He cuffed me once and I hit on a compromise: I nodded my understanding.

A gun grinding cruelly into the nape of my neck. I was on a forced march. Where was he taking me—to his apartment for a nightcap? Not bloody likely.

Now I knew how Howard must've felt.

In fact, I was identifying with Howard on a number of fronts. New York City—seven million of us, right? Yet our attackers (in his case the "attacker" was me) seemed to have no trouble finding deserted locales in which to terrorize us.

No people coming in or out of the many medical facilities lining the streets. Visiting hours were long over. The neighborhood businesses dependent on the hospitals—the delis, the dry cleaners, the florists, the bookstore—all shut down tight. City buses were running maybe one every twenty minutes this time of night. No subway stations at all this far east. If I survived the night, I'd have to write the mayor a nasty letter about that phantom Second Avenue subway.

One thing there was plenty of—for a change—taxis.

The cabs were zipping down York like yellow bugs. Be nice if I could flag one of them down. But my arms remained at my sides. Benson may have been old, but he was moving fast on those long, stiff legs of his. We scooted across the traffic, heading east, moving farther and farther away from whatever life there might have been on the avenue. Farther away from help.

He turned me abruptly to the left, uptown. Maybe we were going to his place after all.

No. At Seventy-third Street he went east again. There was nothing ahead of us but the East River Drive, and on the other side of it, the big water.

Benson was probably going to force me into the fast-moving traffic on the highway. I was going to end up as roadkill on the Upper East Side. How uncool could you get?

To use Aubrey's all-purpose phrase, Fuck this.

I found my woman warrior voice. "I'm going to talk now, Dr. Benson, whether you like it or not."

He started, as if I had awakened him from sleep.

"Listen to me, before this goes too far. You've already killed. But I know what kind of pressure you were under."

"*Pressure?*" he snarled, curled lip and all. "You call what I've been through 'pressure'? I ought to kill you for that alone, you heartless dog."

"I only meant that I know why you did it," I said, trying to placate him. "But this is different. I never harmed you, and you don't have to do this. No matter how much pain you're in, this is plain murder and you know it."

Benson kept piloting me forward, silent.

We were running out of pavement. I was beginning to scent the river and hear the whirr of traffic on the drive.

I'm a talker. I was prepared to bluff and bluster for as long as it took. Either my eloquence would dissuade him from killing me, or I'd have to distract him long enough to get at my gun.

I boomed out: "Hey! Are you listening to me here or what? I know the terrible way Ida Williams betrayed your wife. Lenore thought she was just a sweet little vendor selling dolls at the crafts fair near your house. They liked each other, and Ida became her friend and confidante.

"I know how angry you were when Kevin dropped out of school. When he told you what he wanted to do, it was like he was spitting on your values, trashing you and everything you gave him. He fought with you over money, over his girlfriend, his music—everything. Then he walked out and wouldn't even speak to you anymore. Lenore was vulnerable and close to the breaking point. She turned to her friend Ida. She didn't know Ida was going to betray her. She didn't know Ida was about to drag her down into hell.

"Kevin's death was the most horrible thing that ever happened to Lenore. The only thing in the whole world that was worse? Living with the knowledge that she was the one who killed him.

"Yeah. I got it figured," I said.

And indeed it was a question of figuring. It came together in my head when I realized everybody who knew about the rap wars was thinking in terms of drive-bys. But Black Hat and the others had been killed indoors. They were ambushed as they were about to leave an underground garage. It was easy enough to learn where the garage was located. That's when it came together for me.

"Lenore learned that Junior G, the wildly successful, wealthy rap star that her son worshipped, was living large, right in your neighborhood. Not in the nightmare housing project that he mythologized in his music but on the chic Upper East Side. Everybody was laughing about it. He had just bought a penthouse on the same block as yours. Your wife saw him in the neighborhood from time to time, gold teeth, fur coats, always with an entourage—his posse. She sat on her resentment and hatred of him and everything he represented. Especially she hated that people like him had seduced her son into their worthless, stupid world. Kevin wouldn't even talk to the two of you anymore. It was making her more and more enraged.

"One day she took your gun out of—wherever it is you keep it—and walked a few buildings away and down into the parking garage. There they all were, acting ignorant, loud, smoking spliffs, whatever; piling into that gaudy automobile. She stepped up and emptied the gun into the car, then walked away. No idea Kevin was inside.

"You know this part. I don't have to tell you. Lyle Corwin was in that car. But he wasn't hurt. He got away clean. And he also saw who did the shooting.

"He must've felt like he was solid gold when Felice entered his life. She'd been trying to make you and Lenore cough up money for her foolish ideas about Kevin's music. She was angry that you blew her off. But just imagine how she reacted when Lyle Corwin told her who murdered the boy she loved so much. Felice may not have had a larcenous bone in her body before then, but when

Corwin sold her on the idea of blackmailing your wife, she was all in. She figured you and Lenore deserved whatever you got."

"I didn't know," he said.

"Bullshit, you didn't."

"I didn't know until she'd run through all of her money, and the threats started coming to me at home. That's when they started draining me as well. Bloodsuckers. They were even forging our checks."

"Yep. That's how Lenore realized her wonderful friend Ida Williams was involved. The kindly, wise lady who believed in the spirits. Who hosted ladies' tête-à-têtes with Lenore, serving tea and sympathy. Who listened sympathetically to her terrible confession that she'd shot her own son to death. You had to get involved then. Lenore had run out of money. She had to tell you what she'd done."

"Yes."

"You paid for a while, too. For a while. Maybe just until you located Felice and Lyle Corwin. Ida and her partner were easy enough to locate, so you started getting even with them first."

"I kept all those goddamn dolls so that every time I looked at one of them my hatred would grow stronger. I needed to be strong for what I had to do. I wanted to be face-to-face with that old bitch when I killed her. I wanted to look into her eyes as she died. But I was deprived of that pleasure."

"Couldn't get close enough that night to see her eyes when you shot her? Poor you."

"*I was deprived!*" he screeched. "But that doesn't mean I won't enjoy killing you up close. You and anyone else who would destroy my wife."

"Right. You're the one with all the losses in this thing, right?"

I doubt that he heard me.

"She's worth a hundred of you," he said. "She had been stable for more than fifteen years. She pulled herself out of a mental hospital. She survived miscarriages, injustices, sacrifices you couldn't even begin to understand. But you cannibals managed to break her. Her mind is finally gone."

But . . . is it? I thought. Are you sure about that?

Of course I didn't say those things. I let him go on testifying.

"She's finished now," he said, wiping tears from his cheeks. "She's gone."

"Your wife isn't dead, Dr. Benson. But you know who is? Felice Sanders."

His body seemed to twitch at the mention of her name. He was breathing heavily, enraged. And so was I.

"What's the matter, wise old healer of sick children? What are you thinking about now? Reliving the moment you strangled that girl? Murdered another woman's only child? The moment you turned into a monster yourself?"

I didn't expect an answer. He gave me one, though. "Yes," he said simply.

Then said it again. "Yes. That's what they made me. They turned me into a . . . thing . . . who doesn't care and isn't cared for, who kills without thinking. A dead-end street. That's where all my proud father's sermons and all the trust in my little boy's eyes led me. I left every shred of my pride and fortitude there."

Again, poor old you.

"You had those terrible second thoughts, didn't you? When it was too late. You'll have those same thoughts after you kill me, too, Doc, because you know I'm not part of the stuff that wrecked your life. For Godsake, man, I'm working with the police.

"But you don't care about that, do you? All you know is that *your* family was destroyed . . . *your* money was taken. And your conscience is killing you, isn't it? You'd like to feel all innocent, but you can't. You keep thinking, If I hadn't done this, if I had let him do that, he'd still be alive. I'd still have my son and my wife."

Maybe—just maybe—what I was saying had started to sink in. I couldn't tell.

I began to invent. "Don't you realize the police know all about it now? They're looking for you even as you're doing this. That was Detective Sweet I was talking to."

Benson spoke slowly, his voice goopy like melted ice cream. "I don't care who you were talking to."

"You've been hunting Miller down, haven't you? He's the last one you need to kill. To get even. You won't find him though, because the cops have just arrested him," I lied.

We were now at the point of no return. We'd hit the rock-strewn area just off the access road to the drive. In the summer the place was dotted with the makeshift tents of homeless men. This time of year there were only a few dead pigeons and the sundry detritus of human vice: used condoms, needles, and amyl nitrate vials.

Nothing to lose now, I looked defiantly at the old man. His face was deformed with anguish. "What's this, Doc—more tears? What are you crying about?" I shouted derisively. "I thought you were going to enjoy killing me."

He did try to stop blubbering. He was snuffling and wheezing, trying to calm his breath. He wiped at his eyes with his free hand. But, when he pulled himself together, it wasn't in order to lower the gun and surrender.

Fuck! He was aiming at my heart.

This wasn't right. No, no, no. This was all wrong. I was supposed to live to age ninety and have a blowout weeping-and-wailing Negro kind of funeral like the one in that soapy flick my mom and I watched on the late show—*Imitation of Life*.

That, or I was going to buy it when I missed the hairpin turn in my fabulous convertible on the spindly road high above Saint-Tropez because I'd had too much to drink at *le festival du jazz*.

No, no, he was getting ready to squeeze the trigger.

I exploded in crazed movement. Ducking. Weaving. Running.

His first shot went into my thigh. It felt as if I'd been hit by a train on fire.

He walked toward me, stumbling, sobbing. The next shot missed me.

I knew I'd never make it, but I fumbled for the Beretta anyway. I didn't have any kind of a chance to beat him, my limbs about as useful as one of Ida's dolls'. But I was damned if I'd go out quiet.

Who would've thought I'd be the idiot who assassinated one of the bright lights of African American achievement? Black Excellence, where is you now? Well, I was sure as shit going to, if only I could get off a shot!

Three quick blistering reports settled the matter.

They didn't come from my gun. That was still in my bag.

Benson lay dead, looking awfully surprised.

When I stopped screaming, I heard retreating footsteps. Running.

The dark figure in the dark windbreaker was booking north alongside the access road. I watched him race across the footbridge over the highway at Seventy-fourth and disappear onto the joggers' path beyond.

I knew him. At least I thought I knew him. From somewhere. Who *was* that guy?

CHAPTER 20

BLOOD COUNT

THEY GIVE YOU a cheerful multicolored gown in the hospital these days. I guess they mean well. But I didn't appreciate it. I've always liked plain white against black skin.

I forgave them, though. Fashion mistakes aside, the drugs they handed out were raging. I'd never felt better.

It took a few days for the goof to wear off and make room for the depression that set in.

In the meantime, practically the whole parade of my significant others passed through my semiprivate room. Mom cried the most. Predictably stoical, Pop brought me the most books and magazines. Aubrey brought me the best food, along with a new pair of wildly expensive slippers and a makeup kit full of MAC cosmetics. Dan Hinton's flowers won the prize. He dropped in bearing a load of leopard-skin calla lilies that must have represented a couple weeks' salary for him. My music mentor, Jeff, dropped off some of his wife's fabled peanut butter cookies and a rare Dexter Gordon album that he had run down for me.

One or two other acquaintances passed through. I greeted them all with the same spaced-out smile and stuffed my face with useless calories while they murmured kind words I wasn't really listening to.

Even Detective Loveless came by. But of course that was no courtesy call. He'd grilled me for two hours, never once admitting that I'd been right about Ida's murder from the very beginning.

My people were limited to visiting hours. But Leman Sweet, my single most constant companion, was another story. Leman, being a police officer, was free to come and go as he liked, within reason that is. That suited him just fine, because he had no wish to encounter the rest of my friends and family.

This was one for the books—I was voluntarily spending most of my hanging-out time with Leman Sweet. And, even more amazing, he was about the only person whose conversation held any interest for me. But then, Brother Sweet and I had a lot to go over.

"You ever take a bullet, Sweet?" I asked one afternoon. That day's meds had not yet kicked in.

He looked away and shrugged but wouldn't answer me. Must be some kind of story behind that. I was intrigued, but I didn't pursue it.

Instead we talked about the unbelievable odds at work in these crimes. Chiefly, how often does it happen that two separate blackmailers, who don't know each other, are squeezing the same victim, and then end up working together?

And then the talk turned to Felice Sanders. Leman paid a visit to the girl's mother who, it went without saying, was devastated. I said I was sorry I wasn't going to be able to go to her funeral.

The revenge-obsessed Dr. Benson went to his death with that child's blood on his hands, and probably was never even sure, nor was I, that she had stayed on board with the hounding and blackmailing of Lenore Benson. She might have regretted it as soon as it became real.

Ida was a different story. Dr. Benson *wanted* that murder to be public. Wanted Miller to know he'd killed Ida and take it as a sign he was coming to get him, too.

"Have you done any thinking about how he connected Felice to Miller?" Leman said.

"I think I know," I said. "That night I went to the Bensons' apartment, the phone rang while we were walking down the hallway. Before he picked up, he turned on the desk lamp. There was a caller ID thingy that he looked at. You know, it tells you the name and number of the person calling. It was somebody from the hospital. He talked for a few minutes and then hung up. But when someone else phoned a few minutes later, he looked at the information and decided the call could wait. I thought maybe I heard a man's voice, just for a second, but I couldn't be sure.

"I figure that was Miller calling, and the doctor certainly wasn't going to talk to him while I was there. Benson said that at one time the blackmailers were calling him at home, threatening him and his wife. Probably they'd take care to use phone booths or cell phones or whatever. But this time, the number looked familiar. At any rate, he took note of the incoming number. After I was gone he scrolled back through the call screener and saw it was the same phone that Felice Sanders was using when she called to apologize for acting out at the funeral. The machine told him the number belonged to a family called MacLachlin. One glance at the White Pages and he had their address on Greenwich."

"Not bad, not bad," Leman mused. He couldn't swear to it, but thought there was such a device on the telephone he saw when the cops searched the Benson home. It would be easy enough to check now.

I sat up in bed and picked through the candy selection until I spotted a bittersweet. "The good doctor said that Lenore Benson had a history of mental troubles. Sounded as if she had another really bad breakdown twenty or so years ago."

"Yeah," Leman said, "she did. I got the records from the hospital she was in. After Black Hat was killed, she was holding it together on tranqs and other stuff her psychiatrist prescribed. The pharmacy records show enough scrips to cool out half the addicts in the five boroughs. Plus, come to find out those herbal teas and shit Ida was giving her had some mild psychedelics in them."

"Boy, Ida was good. I was so taken in by her crap."

"I'm reading your mind," Leman said. "You sayin' she was doping Lenore Benson and playing like she could communicate with Black Hat . . . from the beyond . . . or some shit like that. Maybe using those recordings of his that Felice gave to Lyle Corwin. Playin' them like it was her son talking to her again."

"Two things," I said. "First, I actually toyed with that idea. And who knows? Ida and Miller were crazy enough to try some bullshit like that. But no. Even if they did, it didn't work. I was the idiot who was stupid enough to buy into Ida's airy-fairy act. I think Lenore was so much smarter than me—or Ida or Miller. I think she twigged what was happening and she got her gun out and went to Omega that night and put a bullet into Ida's head."

"But you said her husband confessed. He said—"

"He said, and I quote, 'I was deprived.' Deprived of looking into her eyes as she died, because he wasn't there."

I thought about the force of Benson's rage, his blind, lethal rage, and what it must have been like when he strangled Felice. It terrified me all over again.

"Hmm. It could've happened that way, yeah." He was helping

himself to the Jell-O on my lunch tray. "Anyway, you got both lucky and unlucky that last night," he said. "Benson went to the clinic to visit his wife, saw that damn doll, and asked who brought it. They told him you had just left. He was probably hustling up and down York with that doll in one hand and that piece up his other sleeve. Looking in doorways. Just your bad luck, you didn't get right in a cab and come downtown."

"I guess."

"Hold up a minute. You said something about 'two things.'"

"Oh, that. The second is, I'm not sure how crazy Lenore Benson is. I have a strong suspicion that she's counting on not being punished for anything, because of this nervous breakdown. I think it's possible her shrink suspects she's bullshitting, too."

"Huh. Again, something we are not likely to know for sure, ever."

I nodded. "You're right."

"But, man, what kinda angel was looking out for you? A motherfucker shows up out of nowhere, caps Benson before he can cancel your ticket. And we don't have no idea in hell who he coulda been."

"No," I said. "No idea. Maybe Mama Lou sent him."

"You don't believe there's any way it could have been that book seller, do you?"

"Howard? God, no."

"Nah, I don't think so, either. We still got him in custody, but not for much longer. We got no real charges against him."

"Howie just might be bringing charges against me. I was a pretty lousy date. Threatening to castrate him and all."

"He ain't gonna bring nothing," Leman said. "Time I get through with him, he'll be selling hot books in Idaho."

"Idaho." I laughed. "I wonder if that's where that sleazy ass Lyle might be."

Sweet said nothing.

"You know what else?" I said. "I wish Benson had lived long enough to tell me whether he ever caught up with Miller. Did Miller get clean away, like Lyle, or are you gonna start finding parts of him one day?"

"Lyle Corwin's not in Idaho."

I waited for him to continue, but I could only wait a second. "Tell me!"

"He was found dead this morning. Under some pilings off the Morton Street Pier, down in the Village. Took two to the back of his head. Been in the water a few days."

"Ho-ly. Who did it? Doc Benson?"

"I don't know—yet. We got so many goddamn ballistic reports to sort out; so much DNA and prints at that loft in the Village; so many fucked-up crime scenes and so many conflicting stories from Omega . . . But it had to be either him or Miller. And if it was Miller, that means he is in the wind."

My mind began to race. Don't want him in the wind. He is capable of too much mess.

When had Lyle Corwin and Miller last been seen in each other's company? After they almost killed Justin. He saw them as they were clearing out.

So perhaps Dr. Benson did get 'em all. Almost. And he almost got a big-legged girl sax player, too.

We fell silent for a moment, until he asked, "So what's the story with you and that other dude?"

"What dude?"

"The pretty-boy teacher who can't keep it in his pants. I saw him leaving outta here yesterday. I guess he's toast, far as your daddy's concerned."

"Oh, trust me, he is toast burned on both sides."

I felt a pang for Dan Hinton. Who had held my hand very tenderly during his visit. Mom, upon meeting him, already had him fathering my children—no matter how bad he had messed up on the job. They *need* teachers; he can get another job, she assured me.

"Y'all don't have anything going on, do you?" Sweet asked.

Now it was my turn to shrug and say nothing.

"I had a drink with Aubrey the other night," he announced. He ducked his head. "Damn, that Aubrey is a beautiful chick."

"That she is."

"But we're just friends. I decided it was better that way."

It was all I could do not to laugh. I couldn't wait to hear her version of this.

It went that way with Sweet's visits to me during my stay. Piecing the two cases together. Speculating. It was a shame that, after everything that had happened, he was no further ahead on the rap murders than the day I had interrupted his lunch.

THERE WAS ONE OTHER PERSON who provided stimulation—and laughter—for me while I was laid up: Justin.

We talked on the phone every day—he from his hospital bed, I from mine. A thoroughly preposterous state of affairs. I kept him abreast of all my conversations with Sweet. And poor Aubrey spent her days bringing us our mail, take-out cheeseburgers, and, in Justin's case, gay porn magazines. Ordinarily that last duty might have fallen to Kenny, but he had been offered a three-week job in Toronto, and Justin had insisted that he take it.

On the last day of my stay, before Mom and Aubrey arrived to take me home, I made a final call to J.

"Okay, Smash-up. I'll see you soon. I'm already planning a gala celebration at Caesar's. You rescued me, child. We're going to party till the cows come home. I think I'll invite this cute orderly who works the night shift."

"That's a date, J," I said. "And as long as we're discussing the guest list, I just want to ask a question."

"What's that?"

Time to make my move: "Am I going to be dancing with somebody who thinks my name is Thelma?"

There was silence on his end.

"You called in one last favor since you've been in the hospital. Isn't it true, Justin?"

"I told you to leave things alone, but I knew you wouldn't. I couldn't just let you get killed, Smash. I just provided a little extra protection in case Mama Lou fell down on the job."

I knew there was something familiar about that figure running over the footbridge. I knew who had saved my life that night.

"Lefty," I said. "You cashed in all your chips with Lefty. And now you owe *him* big-time."

"One dance with him, Nanny."

"No problem."

"Get home safe, girlfriend."

SAFE AND SOUND.

I was hobbling and wincing, but so grateful to be in my own place again that I didn't care about that.

I got Mom and Aubrey out of there at the earliest possible moment. I needed to be alone.

By nightfall, without those heavy meds, the whole ugly experience had caved in on me. The misplaced trust. The waste. The violence. And the guilt—all kinds of guilt.

I thought I was a big girl, a grown-up. In fact, I had been telling myself that since I was about thirteen. Plainly now, incontrovertibly, it just wasn't true. I must've had some driving need to be mothered by Ida Williams. I must've needed her to be proud of me. I was showing off. And Ida, whatever wrong she had done in the world, wound up dead. She didn't deserve that.

I had been a royal pain to Aubrey, and the world in general, trying to get over the Andre thing. I did all manner of self-destructive shit while managing not to face the fact that he didn't want me anymore. A grown-up woman should know how to accept that and move on with her life. But Crybaby Nan? She turns to a magic doll for the answers.

I am ridiculous.

Still holding on to those dumb resentments over the so-called mistakes my rather clueless pop made. He obviously was never going to be able to tell me how much he loved me until I made the first move. But I was too stubborn to make it.

When the fuck was I going to grow up?

Well, I had wanted to be alone. And boy, did I get what I asked for.

I also felt old. And I didn't like it one bit.

I wasn't so old. Not even thirty. But wasn't I a bit like Jacob Benson? Dismissive, contemptuous of young people like Black Hat. My dedication to the music I love was in some measure my way of respecting my elders. But should I really hate Black Hat's idols and their young audiences? I didn't hate karaoke fans. Jeez, I couldn't wait for white people to take over rap entirely so Negroes would have to invent something else to listen to.

Why do old people take things so seriously? Why do they get all fusty and threatened when the young just want to find their own way?

Why don't you want to go visit Great-Grandpa? Mom had asked me once. I think I was six then. *Because he won't listen to me,* I had said petulantly, *and he smells bad.*

Once again my thoughts turned to Lenore Benson. Now, there was someone truly alone. If she was lucky, she didn't realize it.

I unpacked one of the covered dishes my mother had left

for me, but I ended up scraping the contents into the **trash. I** couldn't even imagine eating dinner.

I stood in the kitchen, dizzy with loneliness.

I felt as if I'd fall off the edge of the earth if I didn't find **some-**thing to hang on to.

So I picked up the two dolls and held them.

CHAPTER 21

SOMETHING TO LIVE FOR

THE TELEPHONE was unplugged. Like it was every night.

As it began, so it would end. Everything the same.

Except for the booze.

Oh, I was drinking some. But not with the same abandon. I was just getting through the days and nights, just doing the time. The girls (Mama Lou and Dilsey) and I settled down every evening with a drink, a book, and the CD we were currently obsessed with: Jimmy Scott. He was old now, and that singular, unearthly voice of his showed it. He had turned his talents to an amazingly quirky collection of songs. Like Elton John's "Sorry." When I heard him do that one, I had to put my book aside and lie down on the sofa.

A commotion in the hallway awoke me about eleven one night. First I heard the voice of the woman who lived with a house full of kids at the other end of the hall. Then I recognized the super's voice.

A minute later there was a knock at my door.

Ridiculous. Who would be coming to call at this hour?

"Get out of here!" I screamed suddenly. "I've got a gun in here. I'm not kidding—I'll shoot."

I sat there in the dark gritting my teeth as the tapping went on and on. It had to be Aubrey and Justin at the door. Coming to cheer me up. I had told them I didn't want to be bothered, goddammit. I did not want to be cheered fucking up.

The super's voice grew louder as he argued with another man. One of them was calling my name now.

I couldn't take it anymore. I switched on the light and lurched over to the door, snatched it open.

I saw the violin case first.

"Nan?"

At last, the definitive proof that I was no hardass, no Femme Nikita—my eyes rolled up into my head, my legs turned to water and—like the girl I was—I fainted.

It was Andre standing there.

"CAN'T YOU AFFORD to pay your phone bill?"

I reached for him, clutched at him like a blind man falling down the subway steps.

How can it be? What's going on? Something told me to wait—to hang on—and I did. Dan Hinton wanted me, and Howard, and Lefty. But I was waiting for you. For you. What took you so long?

I wanted to say all those things, but I couldn't. I couldn't talk. When I finally did speak, something insane came out of my throat: "Horace Tapscott was in town, you bastard! Horace Tapscott! Do you know how long it's been since he was in New York? I didn't go, Andre! I was waiting for you! And now the poor man is dead!"

My outburst left him, understandably, dazed.

I sat there fuming while he ushered the super out.

"Let me get you some water, Nan. Where's the kitchen?"

I pointed. But when he turned to go, I snatched him back. "Andre? It is you, isn't it?"

"Yes, Nan, it's me." He took me by the shoulders. "Look at you. You're nothing but skin and bones, girl. Are you destitute?"

But before I could answer, he got a good look at my crutches propped against the refrigerator. "Jesus, Nan, what happened?"

"Never mind that now. Just hold me . . . tighter than that. You can hold me tighter than that. I remember."

Andre was, if anything, more beautiful than I remembered. I was inarguably a mess. But he did not seem to mind. We made love for hours, careful about my sore leg at first, but then finding a rhythm that accommodated it.

Afterward I hobbled around the kitchen and gathered a few scraps of ham and a stale brownie for him to eat. I made cocoa, spiked it with bourbon, and then put everything on a tray and brought it into the bedroom.

I held on to his back while he ate. I wanted to close my eyes, lay my head against him, but I didn't dare. I didn't dare blink for fear he would disappear in a puff of smoke.

We finished the cocoa and got bedded down for the night.

It was nearly dawn. I was happier than I ever imagined I could be. And so beautifully sleepy. To tell you the truth, I think I might actually have been asleep.

"Andre?"

"What, sweetheart?" he said drowsily.

"First thing tomorrow, will you tell me what Paris looked like when you left?"

"Uh-huh."

"Andre?"

"What?"

"Do you have a gray raincoat? With a tight belt?"

"No. Why?"

"Remind me tomorrow, okay? About Miller. It was Miller."

"Who?"

"You know what else I just dreamed, Andre?"

"What?"

I giggled. "I dreamed you told me you got married. That you have a wife in Paris."

Long pause. Then, "That wasn't a dream, Nan. I did tell you that."

"You lost your hat? I'm sorry, babe. We'll get you a new one."

"Did you hear what I said, Nan?"

"Hmm, you too, my love. See you in the morning."

I kissed him once more, pulled the comforter up, turned on my side, and drifted off.

I slept like a child.